Do Secrets Count as Sabotage?

In memory of my grandma

Helen Salter comes from South London where she spent most of her teenage years waiting for something exciting to happen. To compensate she has been cramming in random activities ever since, including selling aerial photographs door-to-door in Chicago, teaching English to teenagers in Paris and running around Florence working as a tour guide. Helen has found that she needs to sit still in order to write, which works very well as long as she has access to huge mugs of tea and some chocolate for dunking purposes.

Acclaim for Helen Salter's previous books

Does Snogging Count as Exercise?

'You won't want it to end.'
Cathy Hopkins

Does Glitter Count as Camouflage?

'Lively, warm and laugh-out-loud funny'
Chicklish

Do Secrets Count as Sabotage?

Helen Salter

Piccadilly Press • London

*A big thank you to Anne, Brenda and the rest of the marvellous
Piccadilly team, notably Vivien, Margot, Mary and Melissa. Thanks too to
my two-person cheerleading squad, Gill and Louise, for the pep talks
over bottles of Rioja, and, finally, to Andy for his support.*

First published in Great Britain in 2008
by Piccadilly Press Ltd,
5 Castle Road, London NW1 8PR
www.piccadillypress.co.uk

A catalogue record for this book is available from the British Library

ISBN-13: 978 1 85340 952 3 (trade paperback)

1 3 5 7 9 10 8 6 4 2

Printed and bound in Great Britain by CPI Bookmarque, CR0 4TD
Typeset by M Rules, London, based on a design by Louise Millar
Cover design by Simon Davies
Set in Melanie BT, Stone and Regular Joe

Papers used by Piccadilly Press are produced from forests grown and
managed as a renewable resource, and which conform to the
requirements of recognised forestry accreditation schemes.

Mixed Sources
Product group from well-managed
forests and other controlled sources
www.fsc.org Cert no. TT-COC-002227
© 1996 Forest Stewardship Council
FSC

Help!

'They won't cancel PE,' said Poppy.

'They might,' I said delightedly, looking through the window at the pouring rain. We were supposed to be playing netball after maths but we couldn't, surely, not now. We could spend the time doing nice things instead, things we wanted to do. I would go to the library and find something I hadn't read!

I focused back in on the current lesson. How could maths be so full of stupid questions, when there was me and Luke to think about? This was the kind of thing you got asked in maths at Burlington Girls', as far as I could tell:

'John has five socks in a drawer, two red with orange bits and three purple with blue zigzags. If he takes out two in the dark, what is the probability that a) he should turn the lights on and b) he should change his dress sense? (10 marks.)'

1

Things I Could Be Thinking About Instead of What a Fictional Person Called John Puts on His Feet:

1. Luke has officially been my boyfriend for a whole week and we have had nine snogs so far.
2. He has phoned me twelve times (ten times if you don't count when his phone had turned itself on inside his bag by accident).
3. Luke likes my tangly mousey brown hair and says it is 'untamed'.
4. AND lots of people from school have seen him now: Rashida and Bethan saw him with me in town and Susanna has also seen him, but only from a distance (and she is really square so will probably have been shocked, which is really funny).

All that time sitting around wishing something would happen, and it finally had! For our one-week anniversary, Luke even made me baked beans on toast. It was so romantic. I had no idea he could cook!

My friend Sasha leaned across the aisle to write on my maths book. Surprised, I looked to see if she was giving me the answers. Usually it was the other way round: she was the rebel and I was the academic one.

No. She just wrote, 'Hi Holly. Found any flaws yet?'

In pencil, thank goodness. I wrote underneath, 'How did you know?'

She put, 'You've got that dreamy look on your face again.'

Oh. I kept trying to hide that, with little success. It was just as well I had resolved to tell my mum about Luke tonight. It seemed like an easy thing for most people ('By the way, Mum, I'm finally a normal fifteen-year-old with a proper boyfriend'), but my mum was different. I knew she would freak out. Ever since I could remember, she'd always said my older sister Ivy and I were 'too young for all that' and tutted pointedly when TV characters started dating somebody older, or God forbid, 'got intimate'. But I was going to speak to her about it tonight, so that everything would be out in the open, where it belonged.

Fortunately Mrs Craignish announced we had five minutes to work on our group projects, so I seized the moment.

'Luke's perfect,' I whispered to Sasha. Honestly, he was. 'We watched a DVD last night. Before, we went into his kitchen for popcorn and Luke burped just as I hiccupped!'

Sasha looked blank.

'So we are really, you know, in tune,' I explained. 'Oh, and then we ended up having this really funny conversation about cereal!'

For some reason Sasha didn't seem that impressed. 'Maybe you had to be there?' she commented. She raised an eyebrow at Poppy, in her usual position next to me.

'I left them to it,' said Poppy, poking me teasingly with her biro. 'I've already heard all this on the bus this morning. Twice.'

I giggled. Luke was Poppy's older brother, so she couldn't understand why I found him so gorgeous. However anyone with half a brain could tell he was totally irresistible. (Green eyes, curly brown hair, infectious grin – yum.)

Sasha grinned at Poppy then sat back in her seat. They only really knew each other through me. Poppy and I lived on the same street, and she was about as useless with boys as me (well, as I was until the Luke Miracle), whereas Sasha was a bit of a boy expert.

In fact Sasha and I didn't have that much in common any more, as she lived quite far away, but our friendship was, well, tradition. We'd been friends since infants' school! Besides, she turned up at school on Mondays with all sorts of colourful stories about her boyfriend, Darren, while I quietly lent her my homework. It was a kind of exchange.

'Do you want a bit of chocolate?' said Sasha out of the blue. Strange question, really. I was always in need of chocolate, unless stated otherwise. But, still.

'You can't eat chocolate during maths!' I pointed out.

'You can if no one notices,' Sasha said calmly. 'Just a little square.'

'No I'm not!' I said, outraged.

'No – have just a little square.'

I eyed Mrs Craignish, then the bar, then quickly took a bit. Then, for some strange reason, I paused. I suddenly didn't feel like eating it!

'Oh my God, what's wrong?' said Sasha in panic.

'I don't know,' I said slowly, looking at the square of chocolate in my hand. This had never happened before.

'Don't panic, Sasha,' said Poppy nervously, patting me reassuringly on the arm. 'Looking at Mrs Craignish must have put her off.'

'No, it's not that,' I said. 'I'm nervous about telling my mum about Luke.'

'Oh my God!' said Poppy, raising her voice to the extent that Mrs Craignish went, 'Less chat, more probability!'

Mrs Craignish really should have learned to accept us talking by now. It had happened every lesson since, well, forever. Sasha, who was braver than Poppy and me put together, made a scornful 'tssk' noise with her teeth, then promptly went back to our conversation.

'Are you sure you should tell her?'

I nodded bravely.

Poppy and Sasha looked absolutely stricken. OK, they had a point. But did they have to reinforce how scary it was going to be? Couldn't they just, you know, pretend, and say that my mum was perfectly normal and that it was going to be fine?

'I decided earlier,' I said.

'Can't you just lie?' said Poppy.

'I don't want to,' I said. 'I'd hate it.'

'You're so honest,' said Poppy, gratifyingly awed.

Mrs Craignish looked like she might be coming over, so Sasha quickly stuffed the chocolate back into her blazer pocket. Help, I wasn't wearing my blazer. For want of a better place, I hastily shoved my bit into my shoe.

'I'm just an honest person,' I whispered hastily, enveloped by a new, slightly unfamiliar glow of righteousness. It felt really good actually. Mum was about to learn that, although I was not sporty like Ivy or my little brother Jamie, I was adult and grown up. Mum would then immediately reconsider her strange attitudes about boys being a harmful influence! I mean, it was quite clear that things like a big bottom, fixed braces and a lack of pocket money were far more likely to inflict psychological damage.

Even when I was in the locker rooms in my netball kit, I continued to hope PE would be cancelled. I needed to chill out before telling Mum my news. Our PE teacher, Mrs Mastiff, really led me on by starting her sentence with, 'I am pleased to announce . . .'

I held my breath in delighted anticipation, only for her to finish, 'since it's raining, I have arranged for Year Ten PE to be held in the Assembly Hall!'

I am sure she gave me a look of suppressed glee as she said it. Mrs Mastiff hated me. This was in direct contrast to Ivy, who had been, by all accounts, the best pupil in the universe. Although, Mrs Mastiff was the least of my troubles, sports-wise. My family was like a crack four-person sporting elite, resplendent in matching tracksuits, their lives an endless procession of matches, gym sessions and assorted something-athons. I'd never been sporty, ever, despite Mum's persistent and occasionally military-style efforts to get me to fit in. No, ironically I was the middle child, yet about as far on the outside as it was possible to be.

At least I had been allowed to leave the Year Ten cross-country team, to which Mrs Mastiff had doomed me at the start of the year. The school had decided that a few people would do GCSE English in one year instead of two, and me and Susanna Forbes had been chosen out of our class! It meant I could do a different GCSE next year, and end up with more in total. Although it did involve two sadistically-timetabled extra classes a week, one before school on Monday and one after school on Friday, which was:

a) *An immense pain.*

b) *Clear proof that our English teacher, Mrs Mitford, had no life.*

c) *A further illustration that school, lessons, exams etc were nothing but an*

6

elaborate ploy to thwart teenagers' social lives ('Ha – let's make them
stay in and learn about igneous rocks. Oh, and let's give them a deeply
unattractive purple-and-grey school uniform too. That should do it.')

Anyway, Mrs Mastiff blew a ridiculously over-loud whistle (kept on a red shoelace around her neck) and our class began the dash from the locker rooms through the rain towards the Assembly Hall, which was separate from the main building. How annoying. All the nice crunchy autumn leaves had gone slippery from the rain, before Luke and I had even had a chance to run through them (you know, in slow motion).

Poppy and I were being scientific, running in zigzags trying to dodge raindrops. When we got inside, dripping, Mrs Mastiff mercifully let us cluster into teams depending on who we were already standing with, to save time. To be honest, it didn't matter who Poppy and I were with as long as it wasn't Claudia, Poppy's Public Enemy Number One. Some people are just really intimidating, and Claudia was one of them: wealthy, confident and exotic. Well, half-Italian, anyway, which was more exotic than the rest of us, who were just from South London. Oh, and she was a huge boy magnet.

Poppy and Claudia had become friends before, but then fell out spectacularly when Claudia went off with Jez, Poppy's intended boyfriend. After Claudia dumped Jez for her current boyfriend, Mark, she had optimistically enlisted my help to make up with Poppy. Claudia and I were like chalk and cheese, but, to be honest, I hated the fact that school was a war zone. So I had tried really hard to help, but Poppy had stubbornly shut Claudia out.

Luckily, we were doing a relay race, which had a useful design

7

flaw. Basically one line of girls had to run and touch the wall, then run back and pass the baton to the next person in their team's line, and so on. So it involved some waiting about. I was able to mentally polish the plan that I had been refining in my rough book all week:

Basic Plan for This Evening

1. *Luke and I meet at his house and get the bus.*
2. *We sit upstairs at the back, with his arm round me.*
3. *We go to the cinema together, ideally to see something rated 18 (but if not 15 would be OK), and sit in the back row and snog. (Optional extra: on the way out we see a bunch of sad Year Nines who couldn't get into the film and who look really jealous.)*
4. *We walk home with Luke's arm around me, then snog goodbye at my door.*
5. *I listen to music in the dark with my headphones in and fall asleep pretending Luke is my pillow.*

I was just biting my nails (not easy with fixed braces) and thinking nervously about the news I had for Mum, when I noticed Poppy counting who was where. She announced, 'Actually, I'm going to be racing against Claudia. No way!' and promptly dived in front of me.

I paused in my nail-biting and protested, 'That means I have to race her.'

Poppy looked at me pleadingly.

'Oh, OK,' I said.

So after Poppy had run in parallel to our friend Jo from

Claudia's team, it was my turn. Claudia was ahead of me until suddenly, out of nowhere, she dropped the baton and had to bend to retrieve it! As I returned, Poppy's grin of jubilation confirmed the impossible: I had beaten Claudia! Claudia returned and said sharply to Jo, 'You passed that too quickly. I couldn't keep hold of it!' She gave me a filthy look as she pulled the hairband from her mane of dark hair and re-did her ponytail.

OK, so my team didn't win the entire relay, but we didn't come last! I decided it was a good omen for telling Mum about Luke.

As I was walking home from the bus stop with Poppy, I texted Jo: *'Hope you are OK after PE.'*

What I meant was, 'after Claudia being mean'. However, you had to be careful with Jo because she was (bizarrely) friends with Claudia. And I was always really paranoid that I would accidentally send any bitchy texts to Claudia herself by mistake, or that everyone in my phone would receive it in some wildly unfortunate mobile malfunction.

Happily, I think Jo understood because she texted back really quickly with, *'She was just annoyed because you beat her, Jx'*

Hmm. Jo had once told me that Claudia resented me ever since she'd failed to make up with Poppy. It was twisted logic, considering that I had really tried to help her sort things out. Yet Jo still insisted that Claudia could be a really nice person and went on about how generous and dynamic she was.

Then Luke called! Ooh, it was so much fun having a boy-friend – thank you, God. We had a really intense six-minute chat (me and Luke, that is, not God). Six minutes is the longest I can spin out the two-minute journey from Poppy's to my house. It involves taking small steps and stopping to look at fascinating features of the South London landscape: bins, trees, gum stuck to the pavement, etc.

Anyway, Luke and I had so much in common! We liked all the same films! We talked about all sorts of things, like why it is that when you start walking to school, a bus always comes at that precise point, and how there should be more days in the weekend. It was amazing, I never even used to be able to talk to boys, and I had come so far!

Although, after I got off the phone I suddenly felt a bit worried. What if we had just used up all our things-in-common and conversation topics, and now didn't have anything else to talk about? I would have to think of some more and write them down, and –

Suddenly I noticed Dad open the front door and observe my somewhat haphazard approach down the road. Mum was probably with him; she was always behind any monitoring of my whereabouts. Not for the first time, I wondered if she had some sort of surveillance device hidden away somewhere on my school uniform. I stopped feigning interest in bits of gum and started walking at normal speed, trying to feel purposeful. I know I'd had a lifetime of disapproval whenever boys were mentioned, but surely she knew this had to happen at some point? I was going out with Luke tonight. End of story.

I reached the door and unsurprisingly I saw Mum was in the hall behind Dad. Maybe she had roped him in to do surveillance because he was taller. She looked really annoyed. Had a bird made a nest in her netball hoop again?

Then I noticed Dad holding the phone bill. Oh.

'Holly,' said Mum, taking the phone bill from Dad, apparently for no reason other than to wave it around in an exaggerated manner, 'this is much more expensive than usual. And it's got mobile numbers on it!'

Dad tried to take it back but Mum was too busy waving it, so he resigned himself to pointing at it and adding, 'Whose number is on there four times?'

'I don't know, I bet it was Ivy or Jamie!'

I kicked off my school shoes (new, grey, bewilderingly expensive for such a dull item, inexplicably named 'Belinda') in the direction of the shoe rack. Mum sighed. It was so outrageous. She and Dad always thought it was me who had moved the sellotape or the pen from by the phone, as well. And it never was. *And* I only made calls on the landline when my mobile was out of credit, because at least with a mobile you could do your important calls in your wardrobe or other places where your mum couldn't eavesdrop on you mercilessly. I mean, the other day I was on the landline talking to Poppy about a difficult homework question and Mum called out, 'It's Anne Boleyn!' *from the upstairs bathroom.*

So Mum made me stand in the hall while she went through her list of emergency numbers. I bet it was Jamie or his friends Asif and Imran. They are eleven and all quite capable of dialling a phone, although not of being normal human beings. Or maybe it was Ivy, when she was home from doing her Sports Science degree. (Oh my God. I couldn't even imagine the freedom of being at uni. I wouldn't come home for the weekend: I would be far too busy sticking posters of Luke on my wall and eating cake mixture all day.)

11

Finally Mum exclaimed, 'Holly – this is your mobile number!'

Oh. It must have been from when I'd called my mobile in order to locate it in the house. Mum didn't seem at all impressed by my ingenuity! Whoever invented itemised phone bills should be shot. Or at least made to itemise everything in the world, just so they realised how mind-numbingly irritating it was to record every last detail.

So, in the end I didn't broach the subject of Luke. How could I possibly tell Mum about my seventeen-year-old boyfriend, if a few mobile numbers caused apoplexy? I mean, it had been a week; I couldn't pretend it wasn't serious.

I was almost upstairs in my loft bedroom when Mum called out, 'Holly, why does one of your shoes have a bit of melted chocolate in it?'

She sounded a bit angry about that.

Yes. Maybe I would just go out with Luke this one time and then tell her. After all, I was dying to see him. I didn't want to have some kind of pointless argument with Mum and risk messing up my first-ever relationship, did I?

Comfortably Numb

After all that planning, I didn't really get to do as much snogging or Luke's-arm-round-me stuff as I had wanted, because we spent the whole evening with his best friend, Craig. OK, I watched Luke and Craig playing pool. It was still romantic and stuff, but not really quite what I had planned.

I met Luke at his house, and as we set off he said, 'Oh, I thought we could go round to Craig's because he's at his mum's this weekend,' and I said, 'Yes OK, cool,' because I couldn't really say, 'But I wanted popcorn!'

Positive Thinking About Spending the Evening With Craig

a) *Maybe we could watch a film with the lights off at Craig's and it would be really similar to the cinema but not cost any money (which was good because I didn't have any).*

b) *It would be very safe, as we were less likely to bump into one of Mum's friends in Craig's living room than at the cinema.*

Actually, I was quite pleased with the solution I found re: Mum. When I went out to see Luke, she said, 'Where are you going?' and I said, 'I'm going to Poppy's.' Which was true! I was going to Poppy's, just to meet Luke! So, I wasn't actively lying, just omitting to mention a tiny bit of information!

So Craig and Luke played pool for twenty-three billion hours until sadly the black ball shot off the table and got lost, meaning Luke sat on the sofa and put his arm around me (hurrah!). Actually, after a while my arm went a bit numb and I needed to stretch, but it was like when Charlotte's kitten sat on my lap at her birthday party last year; I was so pleased that I didn't want to change anything by moving.

Then the boys decided we would go up to Kestrel Hill so Craig could smoke a cigarette. And as we started walking, Poppy rang me! It was so mad. I had just been going to call her! She could probably sense all my subliminal worrying about being out behind Mum's back:

Things I Was Worried Might Happen, Even Though They Never Had Before

- *What if Claudia told her mum about me and Luke, and her mum went up to my mum at the country club and mentioned it?*
- *What if my mum read some article about street crime and then turned up at the Taylors', wanting to walk me home?*

I opened my mouth but Poppy said immediately, 'How did it go with your mum, was it awful?'

Oh.

I explained that I had been cruelly prevented from telling Mum. 'But it's not bad, really, because we did start at your house. I didn't even really have to lie!'

'What, so she just doesn't know you're not here *now*?' said Poppy.

'Exactly.'

There was a pause and then I added, worriedly, 'Oh God, what if she calls your house?'

'Would she call my landline? Why not your mobile?' said Poppy.

'She sometimes calls my mobile. But she knows your landline number off by heart. And she thinks mobiles are really expensive.'

'You worry too much. There's no reason why she would call. But if she does, I'll make up some reason why you can't come to the phone, then call your mobile so you can ring her back.'

'This is just a temporary situation until I tell her,' I said. 'I promise.'

I put my phone away and slowly tried to relax. Why couldn't Ivy have shown signs of normality and covered this territory first? It was supposed to be a much easier ride for younger siblings. However, Ivy was just as sports-obsessed as Mum and still showing no signs of interest in boys. (Maybe Ivy was a lesbian or something?)

Fortunately it had stopped raining earlier, so Kestrel Hill was only a bit muddy. Kestrel Hill is a park that's open on all sides, so you can still go in at night. Luke and I sat in the shelter at the top of the hill and Craig wandered off until we could just see the little orange tip of his cigarette bobbing about. The shelter had a hole in the roof and was all charred inside after some sort of fire, but we could still sit on the blackened bench and look at the stars. Luke

15

put his coat down so that I wouldn't get reverse graffiti lettering on my jeans, which was really sweet. Then he put his arm around me and pointed out all the light pollution. It was so romantic! I tried to remember every last detail for sharing with everyone on Monday.

Then we talked about what films we had watched when we were kids, and about Great Questions of Life (you know, Great Questions of Life, like, 'If you are not "disgruntled", does that mean you are "gruntled"?') Luke thought of some too! His showed an impressive grasp of the concept:

Luke's Great Questions of Life

1. *Why, as soon as you say out loud, 'I'm going to sneeze?' do you usually stop needing to sneeze?*
2. *Do flies ever go to sleep? If so, where?*
3. *If you put anti-ageing cream on a baby, does it get younger and younger and then just disappear?*

It was brilliant that we could have these really intellectual discussions. Then Luke talked about his film studies A-level and how his group were holding regular film nights as part of their course. Then he complained, 'It's so unfair, though. I wanted to do a work placement. How come Craig got to work in HMV? I am not a happy bunny.'

He paused, then added, 'Although, why is it a happy bunny? Why isn't it, like, a penguin?'

'What, "I'm not a happy penguin?"' I said, giggling slightly. I mean, how sweet is that?

He laughed too and then said, 'Anyway, how are your GCSEs going?'

I told him about how annoying Claudia had been in PE and how she hated me.

'Ignore her,' said Luke.

'Don't be horrid,' I said. 'Really, it's not good, all the tension and stuff.'

'You're too nice.'

Luke had heard all about Claudia from Poppy. Once, Claudia had even flirted with him! Thank God, he hadn't liked her back, having decided she wasn't his type.

We started kissing. Mmm. Before Luke, I didn't really know how good kissing was. I mean, I had kissed someone before, but it had been mainly something to talk about at sleepovers. With Luke, I felt a strong pull of attraction, as if I could get all tangled up in him.

Suddenly there was a distant 'Oof!' sound and the orange cigarette tip plummeted, presumably with Craig still attached.

We paused, lip to lip, and Luke said, 'You OK, mate?' into the darkness.

'Fine,' came a plaintive-sounding response.

'We'd better go before he gets lost or something,' said Luke.

As we stood up, Luke added something amazing.

'You should come to Fireworks Night with my family. My mum can get you a ticket.'

Oh my God. He thought we would still be together on Fireworks Night, four whole weeks away! That was amazing, because I basically kept thinking Luke was going to suddenly turn around and go, 'Er – what is going on? Why am I with you, Holly

17

Stockwell? Away with you, fifteen-year-old with large bottom and tangly brown hair!'

Or something like that anyway.

Ooh, Fireworks Night would be great. It was a nice, normal Taylor family tradition. They all went to the display in the next town, the posh one you needed to get tickets for, with some other families they knew from the youth club we all used to go to. Unlike Stockwell family traditions, it didn't involve:

- *Jumping into cold water and holding desperately onto the side until a kind stranger said you could stop (also known as a swimathon).*
- *Being frogmarched to the site of a rounders tournament, while you observed that the word tournament contains the word 'torment' for a reason.*

And it was silly, but it had always been a big fantasy of mine, to have someone close to me when it was cold and dark, watching the fireworks. I could be looking up at the night sky and Luke would put his arms around me so I was cosy and warm, like getting into a hot bubble bath . . .

As we walked down the hill, I hung back to call Poppy.

'Has my mum . . .?'

'No, no one's called,' she confirmed.

Thank goodness for that.

As I caught up, Luke said, 'We'll walk you home.' You know, as if he had no brain.

'You can't,' I said, panicked.

'Is Craig being too loud?' Luke turned round and yelled, 'Craig!

18

Put. The. Cone. Down,' as if he was an American cop or something.

I giggled, 'No, because—'

'Step. Away. From. The. Cone!'

'Shut up. No, I mean because my mum will see you.' I
explained about how there had been a small problem telling Mum
the exact truth about us going out. OK, I hadn't told her anything
yet.

'You should tell her,' said Luke. 'How hard can it be?'

'I'm simply not volunteering the information,' I said firmly.
'She would only say I'm not old enough. It's just something I have
to sort out.'

'So I can't walk you home then?' Luke repeated, jokily, then
laughed and tickled me.

As I kissed him goodbye, I realised the very idea of all this stopping – of Mum finding out and going bonkers – was almost
unbearable. I decided to just keep my mouth shut for a little while.
(With my family. Not when snogging.)

Stupid Girl

Why couldn't humans hibernate? It was so monstrously hard to get up in the cold and dark. I was sure that if someone suggested this to the Government, they would agree it was a brilliant idea. Secondly, why were GCSEs so hard? Honestly, we had tons of work and tests and stuff. The one good thing about the whole week was that I had by far the most to report when we exchanged our usual weekend news. Charlotte foolishly attempted to match my romantic description of Luke and the light pollution by telling us all that she had been chatted up by a boy she'd met on her bus, but on further questioning it transpired he had been nine and wearing an orange T-shirt. By German on Friday morning, I was mixing up my verbs. I said, 'I ate the house at five past four,' by mistake. Then Mrs Craignish noticed in maths that one of my long division calculations was wrong, which was annoying because I am usually pretty good at school work. (Although, teachers should be prepared for this, really. No one was going to concentrate on long division when it was almost the weekend, were they?) However, I was getting pretty good at Luke-related maths, although it wasn't on the official syllabus:

Luke-related Maths

- *We have now been going out for 2 weeks, i.e. 14 days.*
- *16 more days = 1 month or $\frac{1}{2}$ of a whole year = the ability to say, 'Luke and I have been going out for (a bit of) a year!'*

Art was OK, although Mrs Leyton has all these strange ideas. She walks around looking at our still life drawings while making baffling statements like, 'Look at the spaces between the objects, instead of the object itself.'

This time she skirted around the room and stood unnervingly behind myself and Poppy as we drew.

'Girls, girls,' she said, 'This is too flat and delicate. You need to get some texture in there! Some nuance!'

The problem with art teachers is that you just know they are dying to grab your pencil and do it for you, much better. But Mrs Leyton restrained herself, got a bit of scrap paper instead and proceeded to draw a violent criss-cross pattern on it, plus some heavy, wild scribbles.

'Cross-hatching and texture,' she pronounced firmly, as if this meant anything to us.

On Saturday I slept in. Just for a little while. It was marvellous, right up until midday when Mum came in, holding my trainers, and suggested I went running with her. So I got up, and Poppy and

I ended up going into town with Luke. Both together! It was brilliant, going out with my best friend's brother. Really easy.

We went to McDonald's to start with and Poppy and I got an orange juice (well, one orange juice with two straws, to save money). Then we went to HMV to see Craig.

As Luke strode through the DVD section, Poppy pointed at *Clueless* and said, 'I watched that again last weekend.'

'We've seen that already!' I said.

'Yes, but my usual DVD library was unavailable!'

'Oh – sorry.'

We used to watch my DVDs in Poppy's front room at the weekend. That is, until I'd started going out with Luke.

'Couldn't you have . . .' I tilted my head at Luke's back.

Poppy muttered, 'Shush! No, his are all foreign. I don't know what's good without you there.'

Luke had a better film collection than me. Poppy knew there was a spare key to his bedroom in the under-stairs cupboard, so occasionally in the past Poppy and I had sneaked into Luke's room while he was out. Not that I was going to say anything to him about that!

We found Craig in the World Film section, straightening DVDs. Although it must have been very useful for any future work in the film industry, Craig seemed quite happy to take his break and sit with us on the bench outside the shop. It was nice being squashed up next to Luke as a buffer against the cold wind. (Except for one thing. Luke had this way of stroking my face that I think was supposed to be tender and romantic, but actually was giving me spots. It was too late to tell him, really, he had been doing it for two weeks.)

Poppy and Craig had to sit quite close together too. I hoped Poppy wouldn't get together with him. He was a bit of an idiot. But then again, just sitting close to someone didn't mean anything.

Craig told us that he went clubbing all the time, etc etc. It was a bit boring, until suddenly he said that his dad owned a recording studio!

'Wow,' I said, impressed despite myself.

'You can come along one night if you want,' said Craig casually. 'I go to my dad's on week nights. Any time is fine, really.'

'What's it like?' I said in awe.

Craig said solemnly, 'Pretty cool.'

Oh my God. I tried to ignore the week night thing, which would be a problem. To think that not that long ago my idea of a wild night out was walking to the newsagent's and buying a King Size Twix with my pocket money rather than a regular one! This was a new era in my life. The era of Cool Holly.

Suddenly Luke said, 'Isn't that Claudia?'

It was ridiculous. I didn't even like hearing him say her name. However, he was right. Claudia was passing the shops in the back seat of an amazing-looking black convertible, with the top down! I don't know what kind of car it was, but Luke muttered, 'BMW. Six series.'

'V8 engine, 333 horsepower,' said Craig, looking impressed.

'Is that Claudia's dad driving?' I interrupted, steering the conversation back towards English.

'No, it must be her mum's boyfriend,' said Poppy, peering at the car as it slowed in traffic. Claudia's mum, Vanessa Sheringham, was a glamorous daytime soap opera actress who, after divorcing Claudia's wealthy businessman father, had kept the big house in Lansdowne and also got herself a younger boyfriend.

'Where's her mum?'

'They're probably going to meet her somewhere.'

'Claudia looks amazing,' I said, despite myself. Poppy wouldn't like me saying it, but it was true. In the car, with her hair swept back off her face, she looked like a model.

'She's fit,' said Craig predictably. Then he added, 'But it's really cold to have the top down.'

Was Craig mad? OK, it was cold and windy, but Claudia was in a convertible! Who cared! I felt the usual pang of envy. Her life was like something out of a film.

Craig had just used this to launch into a story about the time his Dad had a Porsche, when I saw Claudia notice us.

'Put your arm round Luke and wave,' said Poppy, giggling.

'No!' I said. 'That's mean.'

'She's mean,' said Poppy, and pointed at me and Luke, making thumbs-up gestures. I had forgotten that Luke and I were all she had to annoy Claudia with. Sometimes Poppy hated Claudia with a little too much enthusiasm for my liking.

'Poppy!' I hissed.

'Oh, come on,' she said. 'It's all I've got to work with! I'm just having a laugh.'

Then a supervisor came out and told Craig to start DVD-straightening again, so he went back in and we all stood up to leave. As the car drove off, I thought I saw Claudia look back towards us, brows furrowed.

'Did you have a nice time shopping?' Mum called out when I got home. Her voice sounded funny. I opened the living room door to find her upside down in a complicated-looking yoga position.

24

'Yes, it was cool.'

'Did Poppy buy anything?'

'No, but it was still fun,' I said carefully.

There! I hadn't actually said a single thing that was untrue. By my reckoning, this practically undid the not-quite lie I'd told about being at Poppy's the other night. I mean, how many people told their parents everything, really?

Manic Monday

If school, lessons and homework stayed this bad, school would soon be empty because we'd all be in nursing homes recovering from the stress. First thing on Monday I thought I'd lost my school tie so I had to leave for school without it. Then Poppy was distraught because she'd woken up thinking it was a Saturday when it wasn't. I managed to talk her round. It is hard to make a Monday almost the weekend, but it is possible if you think about it carefully. E.g. 'It's Monday today, which means tomorrow will be the day before the middle of the week.'

As if that wasn't enough stress for one day, then I realised I had forgotten to do my maths homework! I had to do it on the bus. Some old ladies helped. They were really good at maths and didn't even have their calculators with them!

That evening I was copying a photo of Luke from my mobile phone into my big sketchbook (still life for art homework) when he texted me to say that Craig had invited us to his dad's recording studio on Wednesday night! How cool was that! But midweek? And would it end really late? And Craig's dad didn't live nearby, did he? It was all a bit risky. I wondered whether Poppy would even be allowed to go. Her mum was pretty relaxed, but this was more than just a trip to the cinema.

I considered my options, realistically. Should I tell Mum the truth now? But what if she didn't let me go? That would be unbearable.

I was just thinking about it when Poppy unexpectedly phoned to say she was outside my front door. I took my sketchbook downstairs and she agreed my drawing of Luke looked quite like him! (Well, her exact words were, 'Yes, well, if you sort of half shut your eyes.')

'I can't stay, my mum's outside in the car. We're going to Tesco's,' Poppy added. 'I just wanted to ask if you'd like to come bowling on Wednesday night with me, my parents and my cousins? My dad found a half-price week night offer for groups.'

'Ooh, that sounds nice,' called out Mum from the living room.

Poppy was a genius! She even knew that my mum would be eavesdropping! I winked and said, 'I'd love to. I'll come over at about seven, shall I?'

We said goodbye as if nothing had even happened. I rushed upstairs to call her.

'Thank you so much!' I whispered excitedly into the phone. 'Honestly, that was excellent timing. I owe you one.'

'What do you mean?'

'The bowling alibi thing. Thank you, honestly, you're such a star. Luke will be delighted that we can go to the recording studio. And I didn't even have to think of something to tell Mum.'

There was a silence. Then Poppy said, slowly, 'Holly – I was genuinely asking you to come with us on Wednesday.'

Oh God.

'Sorry. I just thought . . .'

'I thought you were already seeing Luke on Saturday night?' said Poppy.

'I am. But Craig only sees his dad on week nights, so . . . look, sorry. I thought you were covering for us all. Didn't Luke ask you too?'

'No, he didn't,' said Poppy, sounding a bit flat.

How was I supposed to know Luke would only invite me?

'Sorry – so, you're really going bowling?' I faltered.

'Yes,' said Poppy, 'I'm in this strange world called reality. It's really mad. People say they're driving to bowling with their family, and then they actually do it!'

'Your parents are driving you?'

'Yes. Of course.'

Oh God. How scary. What if my parents saw the Taylors' car go past? They would know I had lied! I couldn't even contemplate what would happen if Mum or Dad saw Poppy, and I wasn't with her.

'Can I ask you a favour?' I said, worriedly. 'Could you get them to go the long way round, so you don't have to drive past my house? If my mum sees you all in the car, she'll know I'm not with you.'

28

There was a pause and then Poppy said, 'Perhaps they could still drive past, but really fast? Like, at the speed of sound or something?'

I was just going to thank her for such a good idea when it appeared she might have been being sarcastic, because she added, 'Or I'll just get them to buy one of those cars like in *Back to the Future*, so it will actually go back in time.'

This seemed to be a problem, all of a sudden.

'Why don't you come along to the recording studio?' I said, desperately. After all, I was sure Luke would be OK with it, and I didn't want things to be funny with Poppy.

'No, I don't think so,' she said. 'I'm going bowling now anyway.'

'Look, forget about the recording studio. I'll come bowling,' I said decisively, to hide the fact that I totally didn't want to. 'I'll just meet Luke quickly afterwards.'

Silence.

'Honestly,' said Poppy finally, 'that's complicated. It's not worth doing it like that. Just forget it.'

'If it's a problem, I can see him another time.'

'No, it's not a problem – I'm fine, really.'

'Sorry,' I said again. After that I didn't really know what to say. Suddenly, things were clearly not fine. But how could I fix them? I couldn't offer to go bowling yet again, because Poppy had said no already. I couldn't say sorry again, because she'd already said that she was fine. It didn't seem like there was much else I could do.

29

Oh dear, oh dear. On Tuesday Poppy and I notched up at least twenty minutes' silence on the bus to school. The thing is, was Poppy annoyed or just being quiet?

The Dilemma of What You Think Might be a Bad Silence Rather Than a Normal Silence but You Aren't Sure

1. *You don't want to act all normal or say anything too nice (in case the other person is actually annoyed and you later regret your initial, pathetic niceness).*
2. *However, you don't want to say anything too annoyed-sounding (in case the other person wasn't actually annoyed and you start a whole new, unnecessary argument by mistake).*

So I said nothing, as usual. I don't like rocking the boat. Or the bus. But in PE it became clear that other people had noticed the tension, too! It was raining again, and it appeared some sadist had installed a sort of torture contraption up one wall of the Assembly Hall, with a metal frame to climb up, ropes, etc.

'The PE department got some extra budget!' Mrs Mastiff said with totally misguided delight. 'You can even hang from those upside down!'

'Make it stop,' I murmured to Sasha. (Thank God for Sasha.) 'No, actually, make *her* stop.'

'She's unstoppable,' said Bethan, who you could always rely on to listen to other people's conversations.

What a waste of money. The PE department could hardly be

trusted to buy good stuff, could they? With all the budget the school had used up on this stupid thing, they could have bought loads of good stuff (a hot chocolate machine, more DVDs and books for the library, etc.).

Ivy would have loved something like this, though. Actually she had come home again last weekend, looking a bit distracted. I was beginning to wonder if she was homesick or something. Mum hadn't said anything was wrong, but then again, in Mum's eyes, Ivy was always fine. The perfect daughter.

Poppy was standing with Charlotte and Bethan instead of near me, so I got in the queue with the sporty gang instead. Everyone would surely interpret this as a clever tactical move, because no one would mind if I kept slipping to the back instead of taking my turn.

I thought I had got away with this until Mrs Mastiff said really loudly, 'Is this a miracle? Miss Stockwell Junior without her partner in crime?'

I noticed a lot of curious looks. Poppy and I were always together, weren't we? In fact the only person who didn't look up was Poppy.

At lunch I mentioned the recording studio to Sasha. It was so brilliant, having a proper, actual teenager-type life instead of the social cachet of a seven-year-old! Although, it was a bit awkward. I was half trying to impress Sasha (particularly following her disappointment when I had mentioned that Luke and I got to Level Five on his new Playstation game and she had mistakenly thought we had got to Fifth Base, whatever that was). However,

31

the other half of me didn't want to draw attention to my news, because Poppy wasn't going. So I spoke quietly, but Sasha reacted really loudly.

'Wow, will there be singers and stuff there?' She actually looked impressed. 'Holly, that is so cool.'

'If you see anyone famous, get their autograph for me!' said Bethan loudly from the lunch table behind. 'No,' she added, actually managing to interrupt herself, 'get a photo on your phone and send it to me!'

'Ooh, can I come too?' asked Charlotte.

'Oh – that's what I meant! Me too!' said Bethan hastily.

I looked over at Poppy, who looked away. I felt really bad.

I had to say quietly that I wasn't sure. I couldn't guarantee Charlotte or Bethan access to the studio itself; it would depend how well they knew Craig. And, unfortunately, they didn't. But I promised to take photos and get autographs for people, since I wasn't personally that bothered about celebrities.

After lunch, we were all heading for biology when Sasha said, 'Is there a bar inside the recording studio?'

'I don't know. Why?'

'If there is, won't you need fake ID to get in past the bouncers?'

Oh God.

In biology I sat silently facing the front taking notes like a robot, while I considered whether I needed fake ID. I didn't have any fake ID. I was only fifteen. Would bouncers be able to tell? Until now my life had just been boring sleepovers and stuff. If only I'd known, I would have been preparing for all this debauchery!

Meanwhile, Mrs Shah was going on about how biology was

important in human relationships and how we all release pheromones. She said mothers have a special bond with their child due to pheromones that come off the top of their head (or something). And then there are pheromones that you subliminally smell when you get a boyfriend. Apparently you are designed to like the way their armpits smell. Yuk! I like the smell of Luke's aftershave, but it's a bit gross to think about sniffing his armpit, to be honest. But I had to write it all down because Mrs Shah could see my page.

'Any questions?' said Mrs Shah.

I felt like putting up my hand and saying, 'Seriously, do I need fake ID? I still have braces, for God's sake. I can't even ask to borrow Sasha's because she is black and I think they would notice that I am not.'

But I didn't.

Walk on the Wild Side

Panic. Panic. It was Wednesday night, twenty minutes before I needed to go out, and I had to get older. Well, technically I was indeed getting older with every minute that passed, but I needed something slightly quicker. I needed to *look* older. But who could I ask for help? Poppy seemed annoyed with me. Charlotte and Bethan both now thought I was cool and I didn't want to disillusion them. Sasha would just tease me gently about being square. Ivy could have lent me something, because we actually shared the same light brown hair (and big bottom, although hopefully such details are not recorded on fake ID). But she was at uni.

I went to get a calming hot chocolate and my gaze alighted upon Jamie at the kitchen table. He was drawing a picture of a footballer, his tongue stuck out in concentration. It was not promising advice territory, but this was a crisis.

'Jamie?' I said, sitting down with my drink. 'What sort of thing makes people look older?'

I could practically see the cogs in his brain whirring around.

'Grey hair,' he said eventually. 'Like Dad.'

'Not that old,' I corrected hastily.

'Wrinkles? Taller?'

'Not that old!'

'I can ask Mum?'

'No, no, taller, that's a good point,' I said, so as not to hurt his feelings, and wrote it on my hand using one of his felt-tipped pens. Back upstairs, I considered my options. OK, so getting taller was not a bad idea. But I only had twenty minutes. Although, I had some of those pads that were supposed to go in a bra. I could put them in my shoes?

Eventually I decided to tiptoe instead, because I kind-of needed the pads for my bra. (I am not like Claudia, who can't even see her own feet.) It was quite promising. I practised by walking around the room a few times, and the third time I didn't even fall over. Tiptoeing gave me a slightly funny walk, but if I stood behind Luke and Craig, only the bouncers would see, not Luke or Craig. Easy!

I told Mum, 'I'm going out. See you later,' and she said, 'Enjoy bowling!' So I wasn't lying, that was just her assumption. Brilliant!

Evidence I Was, Finally, Living on the Edge

1. *I, Holly Stockwell, was going to a recording studio with my seventeen-year-old boyfriend! Someone could try to give me drugs or ANYTHING!*
2. *Even Sasha was impressed, and she is Very Cool!*
3. *It was a week night!*
4. *I hadn't even finished my maths homework!*

After all that, the recording studio was not quite what I had expected. In fact, it appeared to be a keyboard, a microphone and a pair of speakers in Craig's dad's garden shed. I was possibly a bit overdressed in my best black velvet dress and my heels.

Craig did, however, turn the light on and off really fast. 'Like a strobe light,' he explained.

Luke nodded in veneration, so I nodded too. Maybe it did seem quite like a nightclub or something. Not that I have ever been to one.

However, it was still really good because then we went outside into the garden. Craig ran round in circles making chimp noises and doing karate kicks, while Luke put his arm around me and we had a snog (yum).

After a bit, I pulled away slightly so I could talk. 'Is having Craig a bit like having a pet?'

'He is quite hairy,' said Luke thoughtfully. 'He could probably do with a lead.'

'Or one of those little harnesses that toddlers have.'

Luke tightened his grip around me again. I felt all snug. He murmured, 'You know how kids have both gloves on a cord?'

'What, threaded through their sleeves so there is one hanging out at each end?'

'Yes, that's it. I still need that. I lost one of my gloves the other day, it was well annoying!'

I smiled up at him. 'I bet you were cute when you were little.'

'I was.'

I gave him a mock punch. 'What was your first ever word?'

'I don't know.'

'That's three words.'

36

'Ha ha.'

'Ivy's was "Mum".'

'What was yours?' asked Luke.

'Don't know. I doubt they remember.'

'Actually, I think mine was "ball",' said Luke thoughtfully.

Craig was staying at his dad's, so Luke and I finally got to be alone on the train back home. I actually texted Poppy, despite her stroppiness, to check she was OK. I felt bad about her going bowling with just her relatives. Then Luke and I had the biggest snog ever! After a bit, he sort of moved away from kissing my mouth and kissed my neck instead. This gave me a bit of free time to see that everyone on the train carriage was looking at us. (Probably wondering how I had managed to get a boyfriend as gorgeous as Luke.) Then suddenly, with no warning, Luke put his tongue in my ear! It was a weird combination of feeling it and hearing it at the same time, all slurpy – not just a delicate ear-nuzzle, but a full-on rotating-of-the-tongue as if he was trying to get to my eardrum! I had thought maybe Luke would one day put his hand up my top or something (maybe not on the train), and I could then agonise over how far to go, etc etc, and write lots of notes to people about it in German (in the lesson, not *in German*). But instead, I was sitting on a train with a wet ear.

I couldn't really pull away, I didn't think it would be polite, so instead I let him. Until he pulled away and said, 'Why is your face all squished up?'

'I'm fine!' I said, thinking, Oh God. Was it, like, a joint thing and I was supposed to do the same to his ear? I didn't know if I wanted to, really, and how was I supposed to stretch my tongue that far? I looked round the train carriage, wildly looking for an answer or someone who would help, but now they were all sat there looking amused.

'Come on, you can tell me. You can say anything to me, you know that.'

I lowered my voice. 'OK, then – sorry, I don't really like it.'

'What?'

'That. The ear thing. It . . . tickles.'

'Oh.'

And then Luke got into a big strop and didn't say anything for five minutes! A few of the passengers were now looking at me sympathetically. I felt like saying to everyone, Well, I don't know, do I? I haven't had a proper boyfriend before! I guess I was supposed to lie.

When we were nearly back, Luke said in subdued tones, 'I'll walk you home.'

I had to say that I still hadn't quite told Mum about him yet. However, I explained about my brilliant method of avoiding lying. E.g. next time I was planning on saying, 'I am going out with the Taylors,' so the only thing making the sentence untrue would be the difference between single (one Taylor, i.e. Luke) and plural (i.e. multiple Taylors)! And I emphasised that considering the difficult circumstances and how impossible my mum was, I really could have been telling proper lies.

Luke didn't seem as impressed as I thought he would be.

'How hard can it be to talk to her?' he said. 'I just prefer – you know – for everything to be out in the open.'

I felt a surge of affection mixed with irritation. He was so straightforward and honest. But couldn't he see how hard this was? I guess his parents were really relaxed, so he didn't understand.

I kissed him goodbye just before the streetlight by our next-door neighbour Mrs Heathfield's house, which I know is the last spot you are safe if you are looking out of the windows in my house. I sprinted the last bit, worried because Poppy hadn't replied to my text message earlier. What if Mum had seen the Taylors' car going past without me?

But when I closed the front door, she just called out, 'Was bowling good?' and before I could reply she added, regardless, 'It's good you went down there with Poppy's parents. That bowling alley is a bit rough: there are always gangs of boys hanging around outside in hooded tops.'

'What, and they might kidnap us, or force-feed us drugs?' I said, sticking my head round the living room door. Mum wasn't doing a yoga pose today, she was reading some sports magazine (probably *What Racquet?* or *Yoga Poses Monthly*).

'Don't be silly,' said Mum, though it was clear that was what she had meant. 'Oh, and put your shoes away tidily in the hall.'

It was all I could do to not run to the bowling alley and talk to gangs of boys in hooded tops, out of sheer annoyance.

Hurrah, though. Mum had barely let me get a word in edgeways! Yet again, I had cleverly avoided a proper lie.

Under Pressure

As I told Charlotte and Bethan the next morning, the recording studio had been great. And Luke was lovely! (I didn't mention the ear-snogging incident.) And now it was Thursday, which meant only twelve more lessons until Friday night, when I could see Luke again! (Normally fourteen, but I'd missed French and English today because Dad took me to an orthodontist appointment!)

I felt bad about Poppy, so I decided to tell her, in confidence, about the ear-snogging. Then we would laugh about it together and it would reassure her that things were still normal. Genius! As preparation I pulled a face at her during art, after Mrs Leyton had told me that a picture of Luke was not valid as a still life (outrageous!) but Poppy didn't see me.

We were all getting our coats for morning break, when something unbelievable happened.

I heard Poppy's distinctive giggle from over by her locker. I was just going to stick my head round the corner and say, 'What?' when I heard another voice exclaim, 'I know! Boys, eh?'

Oh my God. It was Claudia! Poppy was speaking to Claudia again? Without any warning? How? When? Why?

I couldn't believe it. But it was true. They were giggling away merrily in a huge, exaggerated display of friendliness, as if nothing had ever happened!

'And,' Claudia continued, 'his mum lays out his uniform for him every morning! He is so useless!'

Who? Who was useless?

Poppy said, 'And what about that bit of blond hair that always sticks up at the back? No matter how much gel he puts on it!'

Oh my God. Jez! The very person they had fallen out over! Rather than depicting him as the boy for whom Claudia had betrayed Poppy, they were making it sound as if he was a small, furry kitten who kept getting stuck up trees.

Then Poppy said, 'I told you we should have driven past his house after bowling, that would have been so funny!'

I am fifteen. I am grown up.

Therefore, I waited until Poppy and I got the bus home to say, in a dignified manner, 'Bethan mentioned you went bowling with Claudia?'

That is the plus side with Bethan: she is a total gossip, so you can effectively claim you just got any information from her.

'Yes, that's right,' said Poppy.

I am sorry, but you don't hate someone's guts, start hanging out with them again behind your best friend's back – the one who

41

stuck up for you during all the trouble – and then just say 'Yes, that's right.' It is not acceptable.

'I thought you weren't ever speaking to her again?'

'I wasn't,' said Poppy, feigning interest in the passing shop signs, 'until Tuesday afternoon.'

Tuesday? She'd been speaking to Claudia again for almost two whole days and I was only hearing about it now? No way was I telling her about the ear-snogging now!

'Look, Holly, I know,' Poppy continued. 'But I saw her in the locker room, looking sad. She was right by my locker. I could hardly ignore her.'

Sad? Claudia hadn't looked sad when glaring at me after the relay race. Or from the back of the cool black convertible. And why was Claudia looking sad by Poppy's locker when there were plenty of places in school where you could go and look sad in private?

'She was upset about splitting up with Mark,' said Poppy. She said this as if I was being mean, when it was Poppy who had been calling Claudia turd-face for months, while I tried to calm her down.

'Mark, who she dumped Jez for?'

'Yes. She ended it. He wasn't coming back from uni enough to see her.'

'Look,' I said. 'If you were in a stress about Luke—'

'I wasn't!'

'But I'm sorry if—'

'Look. Holly. We don't have to spend all our time together, do we?'

'No,' I said carefully, as if I was calming down a terrorist who had a hostage. I didn't want to sound like some kind of possessive, nutter-type friend who expected to have a best friend and no one else was allowed in. It honestly wasn't like that at all. It was just that Claudia was so . . . slippery.

Poppy pursed her lips and looked out of the bus window again, so I turned away to face the front. I couldn't help but feel that Poppy was getting back at me by reigniting her friendship with her worst enemy. OK, I had made a teeny, tiny mistake by spending so much time with Luke, but what was this? 'Do Everything Right Or Else' world? Claudia had well and truly spotted her chance.

Then Poppy said, 'Aren't you pleased? You're the one who wanted us to make up.'

So I said hurriedly, 'Of course I'm pleased. It's great! I'm just surprised, that's all.'

Pause.

Then, in case I hadn't sounded pleased enough, I said again, 'It's great! Brilliant!'

Obviously, I was delighted about Poppy and Claudia. Delighted. I thought it through after school in Extra English on Friday, while Mrs Mitford talked about Harper Lee. We were doing *Julius Caesar* with the rest of the class, and *To Kill a Mockingbird* in the extra lessons.

As I concluded, everyone was nice and mature. Things were now straightforward and out in the open. Talking to Claudia again was precisely what I had been pushing Poppy to do, wasn't it?

Although, I had kind of thought that if they ever got back on speaking terms, I would be in the middle of it, convincing Poppy to sort things out and bringing them back together. You know, like some kind of saint. Then Claudia would have been really grateful and everyone would have seen how selfless, diplomatic, big-hearted and generally wonderful I was.

But of course, it was fine like this. And anyway, it wouldn't last. No way. It was like in films where people do a sort of rubbish suicide attempt and actually it was just a 'cry for help'. Poppy talking to Claudia again was a 100%, blatant cry for help. Acting like she was mates with Claudia again, just to get my attention, seemed about the biggest cry for help Poppy could possibly give.

Maybe it wouldn't hurt if I invested a bit more time in seeing Poppy.

So, when Luke phoned that evening, I was strong.

'Meet us in the park,' he said romantically. 'I'm at Craig's. He's going to try to buy cider, and we can sneak into the park and sit on a bench.'

'The park isn't locked.'

'There's one down the road that is locked.'

'Why not just sneak into the unlocked one?'

'That wouldn't be sneaking in, then, would it?'

Either way, I had to disappoint his plans for a romantic evening.

'Sorry, I said I'd work on the biology homework with Poppy.'

That was just an excuse. (In fact, I had phoned her the other day, before the whole Claudia thing, to see if we could make sense of it together. However, Poppy had confessed she definitely didn't know the answers, because she had fallen asleep halfway through

44

the lesson. So we decided that we should organise to fall asleep in alternate lessons, so one of us always had the notes.)

'It's Friday night!' protested Luke.

Pause.

'What are you doing?' he continued. 'I can hear rustling.'

'Nothing,' I said. Actually I was blu-tacking my Luke portrait onto the sloping loft-room ceiling above my bed. Initially I was concerned about Mum seeing it, but Poppy had said that I didn't need to worry, because even if my mum saw it, she wouldn't recognise it was Luke.

'I was just thinking I haven't seen much of Poppy lately,' I continued. 'She'll be at home on her own tonight. I think we need a girls' night in.'

Luke sounded confused. 'It's only Plop. You see her all the time.'

'Yes, but only on the bus and stuff, these days. Anyway, I can see you tomorrow, can't I?' I said valiantly. I was dying to see Luke, actually. Twenty-four additional hours to wait! But it would be worth it to get things back on track with Poppy.

'Actually, I've got that A-level film club this Saturday night. And next Saturday too.'

'Oh.' My heart sank. Luke had already mentioned it and I had forgotten. It was the weekend – my cherished, looked-forward-to weekend – and I wouldn't see Luke, not properly, for a whole further week! A whole thirty-five more lessons with no snogs to rewind in my head! I could have cried.

No, this was important.

I needed to fix things with Poppy.

So, the good part of my brain said to the other part (in a firmer tone than usual) that Luke would still like me if we didn't do any snogging for one week, and I said, 'No, sorry. I still need to see Poppy tonight.'

'OK, that's fine. I'll just see Craig, that's cool,' he said, sounding forlorn. Luke, forlorn about me, Holly!

I called Poppy and suggested a sleepover. She sounded surprised but said, 'Oh, I thought you were seeing Luke! Hang on, I'll just ask my mum!'

After a minute she said, 'Yes, come and sleep over! We're just watching TV!'

She was watching TV with her mum on a Friday night? I felt pleased with my decision. I was saving her from a very sad night indeed.

I Don't Want to Miss a Thing

The first bad sign was the posh string-handled shopping bags in Poppy's hall.

The second bad sign was sitting on the sofa.

Apparently 'we' hadn't meant Poppy and her mum. Apparently 'we' now involved Claudia.

I thought back to Claudia's moment of apparent vulnerability in the school locker rooms. Then I watched her snuggled under Poppy's mum's grey fleecy blanket, eating all the pink marshmallows from a big bag. She didn't look that vulnerable now.

I felt a wave of irritation. I'd made one false move and here she was, back like . . . a rubber band, or something.

I sat down uneasily on the single armchair. I couldn't sit in my usual space on the sofa, because Claudia was in it.

'Are you sleeping over too?' I asked her. As I spoke, I realised this was the first time I'd talked to Claudia for ages.

I was expecting her to be really frosty, given that I knew she hated me. But, strangely, she seemed absolutely fine.

47

'Oh no, I just came back after school for some tea. I'm going home in a bit.'

It was all the fault of Extra English. If I'd got the bus home at the normal time, I would have known about this, and been able to . . . well, sulk a bit earlier.

Claudia added immediately, 'How's it going with Luke? Let's hear all the juicy details!'

The thing was, no way was I gushing about Luke too much. But I didn't have anything negative to say, either. And even if I did, I wouldn't tell Claudia!

So I said cleverly, 'Things are fine. Tell you what though, my mum is a nightmare!'

Ha! I could avoid talking about Luke directly. I told them all about how, apart from Ivy, no one in my family knew about Luke. I mentioned all the hassle of talking in my wardrobe every night (standard anti-eavesdropping manoeuvre) and arranging to meet Luke at the Taylors' house because he couldn't knock at mine.

Claudia said, 'Well, it's so cool that you and Luke are together now. It's a shame you didn't get together in the summer.'

'What, because he was with Lorraine?' I asked, scandalised that Claudia would mention it. Luke had momentarily got together with this girl Lorraine while I was at summer camp with Poppy. It was not something I wanted to be reminded of.

'No, of course not!' said Claudia, doing a shocked face. 'I just mean it's a shame you didn't get together sooner. It's nice to be with someone in the summer, because you get to flirt in the sun and wear bikinis and stuff.'

Claudia clearly only thought this because she looked so stunning in a bikini. She filled one, for starters. (I once said that to Sasha, and she was quite sweet because she said valiantly, 'Holly, you fill a bikini!' I was forced to respond that Claudia filled one in the correct places, i.e. not the bottoms.)

I thought about it and replied, 'It's nice having somebody in winter, too. When it's getting darker, you've got someone there to hug and make you feel all warm and secure, like you belong.'

Poppy looked thoughtful as she stood up. 'Oh, I get that feeling sometimes,' she said, 'when I come home and it's raining outside, but nice and dry inside, and my parents have put the heating on. Do you know what I mean?'

'Not really,' said Claudia. I expect the heating was on all the time in her house.

With no proper warning Poppy left the room, presumably to get drinks. What, she was leaving me and Claudia alone together?

There was an uncomfortable silence. It was abundantly clear neither of us would have been socialising if it hadn't been for Poppy.

Then Claudia suddenly opened her mouth and said, 'I was really upset about splitting up with Mark, you know. Poppy and I just got talking again.'

It was as if she was justifying her presence!

'I know,' I said, slightly surprised.

'We *were* friends before,' she insisted. 'Me going off with Jez was a long time ago. And I've split up with him now. Poppy and I shouldn't let a boy come between us.'

'I know,' I repeated. I felt a bit uneasy, as if this was some sort of PR campaign. It was the same spiel she had given me about the whole situation back at the start of term.

'I did try to help you before,' I said, defending myself a bit. 'You know, when she wasn't speaking to you.'

'I know you did,' said Claudia.

I wondered why Claudia had wanted to make up with Poppy so badly. Maybe Claudia wanted to be friends with people she could feel superior to. Or, maybe she hated knowing that someone was annoyed with her. After all, Claudia wanted universal approval. That was probably it, because otherwise Poppy was just so . . . normal. Most of Claudia's friends, like Cool Tanya from the year above, were all older or cooler or something-er than the usual Year Ten student. (Unless it was precisely *because* Poppy was so normal? Maybe normal was a novelty when you lived in Claudia-world.)

As Poppy came back in holding glasses of orange juice, Claudia said, 'Anyway, so is it actually serious with Luke?'

'We're going to Fireworks Night together in November,' I said defensively. 'And I'm seeing him next Saturday.' Well, actually we hadn't arranged anything yet. But how dare she imply it was just really casual?

Poppy handed me a glass and said, 'Holly, you know there's a fairground at the firework display? You'll have to go on the Big Wheel with Luke. It will be so romantic! Oh, and we'll all have jacket potatoes if it's cold.'

'What's that?' said Claudia.

Poppy explained, 'Oh, it's just this tradition. When we were younger, all the kids from the youth club used to get cold hands, so Mum makes jacket potatoes wrapped in foil. They keep your hands warm during the display and then you eat them afterwards.'

'Wow, that sounds great,' said Claudia, almost wistfully. Strange, because she wasn't even a big fan of carbohydrates.

'Talking of warm hands,' I said, 'Luke was so sweet the other day. He said that he still needs his gloves threaded onto a cord, like you have when you're little! You know, to stop from losing them!'

Drat. As soon as the words were out of my mouth, I was annoyed with myself. I hadn't meant to talk about Luke. It had just slipped out.

'That is really sweet!' said Claudia approvingly. She turned to Poppy and said, 'Aaah.'

I was pleased, despite myself. There was always this irritatingly intoxicating side to Claudia. However annoying she was, you always felt like you wanted her approval.

Meanwhile, I tried to ignore a new issue. I needed to go to the loo.

You would think needing the loo was a simple enough matter, but at sleepovers you had to be very careful. Everyone knew this. You could guarantee people would talk about you while you were gone. What if I left Poppy and Claudia alone together and Claudia said something mean about me?

So I kept smiling and held it in, while Claudia started talking about this new yoga DVD she had been doing.

'In fact, you should come over next weekend and we'll do it!' she said to Poppy. 'My mum's away at the moment, so I can do what I want. It'll be fun!'

I tried to keep my face looking the same on the outside, despite this outrageous breach of etiquette. It is against the law in England to be talking to two friends and make a spontaneous plan with just one of them. (Well, it should be.)

51

'Holly, you could come too,' said Claudia unexpectedly, 'but you don't like yoga, do you?'

'No, I love yoga!' I said hastily, ignoring Poppy, who gave me a funny look.

Claudia looked taken aback. 'Oh! Cool! Well, Auntie Maria's out next Saturday night so we can move the furniture in the living room and get the mats out.'

I gritted my teeth.

'Claudia – Saturday is when Holly is seeing Luke,' said Poppy.

'Oh!' said Claudia. 'Sorry – that's the only day we can do it, really.'

Why? Why had I said I was seeing Luke that Saturday? To make things even more annoying, I had remembered he actually had his film club. So I was free! Not that I could admit that now without looking really stupid.

'I can see Luke Friday night or Sunday daytime instead?' I said quickly, mentally cursing my idiocy. There was no way I was giving Claudia the chance to say I was prioritising Luke over my friends.

'No, no!' said Claudia, 'Honestly. Keep to Saturday. We understand don't we, Poppy?'

I smiled extra broadly to hide my unease.

Then, unfortunately, Poppy went, 'Oh I need the loo, back in a mo.' Claudia and I both leaped up and said, 'Me too!' in a mad fashion. Clearly we didn't want to be alone together. And neither wanted the other to talk to Poppy while out of the room, leaving the remaining person alone like an idiot.

It was a bit ridiculous though, because all three of us ended up traipsing upstairs to the bathroom, all at once, with neither Claudia nor I prepared to concede any ground. Poppy gave us both a funny look as she went into the bathroom. Claudia and I stood on the landing, leaning on opposite walls. It felt like a chess game or something, with people making moves really carefully. After Poppy came out, Claudia and I did all this 'After you, no – after you!' stuff, both pretending we didn't care who would get back first and say something mean behind the other one's back. In the end, Claudia actually accepted one of my fake protestations of politeness and went in before me. Cow!

When she emerged, she dashed downstairs really fast. So I gritted my teeth, went to the loo more quickly than I ever had in my whole life, and plummeted back down the stairs into the living room. When I got back in, Claudia didn't appear to be whispering mean things in Poppy's ear or anything, but who could tell what she had been saying five seconds previously?

Finally we got to the end of the night when Claudia was going to go home. Ha!

That is, until Poppy's mum came in and said, very inconsiderately I thought, 'Claudia, will you be sleeping over too?'

No! No!

Claudia hesitated prettily.

'Come on,' said Poppy's mum with completely unwarranted kindness. 'I've got a spare duvet of Luke's you can borrow.'

I felt that since he was my boyfriend I would have had a complete and utter right to object at that point. Everyone was very lucky that I had three marshmallows in my mouth. What was all this about? Poppy's mum was really nice, but she hadn't paid any particular attention to Claudia before. It wasn't because Claudia's mum was famous, surely?

Before I could even swallow my marshmallows, Claudia had

gracefully accepted and Poppy's mum had sorted out Luke's duvet from the airing cupboard.

'Would you like a pillow?' she asked.

What next, gold?

'Yes, thank you, Mrs Taylor,' said Claudia.

So we all slept over. It went OK, except Claudia kept making statements about how it was great that Luke and I were getting to spend so much time together, and how my life must seem so much more exciting than before, and how it had been a bit of a mission, hadn't it, trying to get Luke for so long? Thank God she was so busy talking that she didn't hear him coming back in at about ten p.m., or she would probably have dragged him into the room to talk to us.

I had a headache when I woke up. I must have fallen asleep with gritted teeth.

Blue Monday

I was reduced to doing homework on Saturday night, since Luke was out at film club. I hadn't even seen him at breakfast on Saturday morning because he had still been asleep when Claudia and I had left (me on foot, Claudia in a taxi – presumably in case she got mugged in our dodgy neighbourhood).

I kind of thought Poppy might phone me on Saturday afternoon to apologise for inflicting Claudia on me on Friday night, but she didn't. I ended up phoning her to see if she wanted to go up to the shops together.

As we were in the newsagent's choosing drinks, I said casually to Poppy, 'What was that all about, your mum being ultra-nice to Claudia all of a sudden?'

Strangely Poppy didn't seem bothered by Friday night's underlying tension. In fact, she seemed happier than she had been for a while!

Poppy looked round as if assessing the area around the drinks fridge for spies (possibly a bit over-dramatic considering the shop was empty apart from us and the man behind the till). She whispered, 'Claudia told me and my mum some stuff at bowling.'

'OK . . .' I said, a bit puzzled.

'Just because you don't share stuff with your mum doesn't mean other people don't,' Poppy pointed out, looking at my face.

I must learn to hide what I am thinking. And also, was it just me or did Poppy seem a bit defensive? I bristled a bit. Did she think I couldn't keep a secret? I studied a can of lemonade to hide my irritation.

'Is ginger beer alchoholic?' said Poppy.

'No.'

'Oh.' She put the can back into the fridge, looking mildly disappointed.

I went quiet on purpose, to see if Poppy would say anything else. When we were paying at the till, my strategy paid off.

'Claudia's feeling really vulnerable right now,' Poppy said suddenly.

'Why?' I said. I tried not to sound suspicious, but it was difficult.

'Well, her mum's gone away filming, hasn't she? She's in Italy. All Claudia's got is her Auntie Maria staying. And Cool Tanya and her other friends from Year Eleven are really obsessed with their exams and coursework this year. So my mum feels sorry for her. She's said to Claudia that she's welcome at our house any time.'

'But Claudia's been going on to Bethan about how great it is being able to have friends round all the time!'

'You know what she's like. At school she only talks about gifts and holidays and stuff. But she's pretty upset. Don't tell anyone, it's a huge secret.'

56

'I promise,' I said, wondering why Claudia had told Poppy's mum if it was such a big secret.

On Monday morning I was walking towards the bus stop, half asleep as usual, when something terrible and unexpected happened. A bus was at the stop so I ran for it, but it was pulling away. That was when I saw Luke was on it! He was upstairs sitting by the window.

So, I stopped running and waved.

And he saw me. He did, he saw me. But he didn't smile!

It was awful.

I tried to call him immediately, but it went through to voice-mail!

I felt sick to my stomach. First he'd seen me and not smiled, and then he had turned his phone off. Why? Didn't he want to speak to me? He had looked all stern, as if something had changed.

I felt so distraught that, contrary to school rules, I didn't hand my mobile phone in during morning registration. I needed it to text Luke before the first lesson. Then, I could covertly check my phone during morning break, by when he would have texted me back.

But at morning break, there was nothing. I must have looked really distraught because even Claudia said, 'Are you OK?'

All I could manage was, 'Fine,' which everyone knows means nothing.

The late morning passed in a miserable blur. Worse than a normal Monday. Throughout German and English, all I could think was, hadn't Luke seen my missed calls? Why hadn't he replied to my voicemail?

There was nothing at lunchtime, either. Could he have run out of battery? Or been mugged and lost his phone? Or broken it somehow? You know, so the voicemail could still receive messages but the screen had cracked or something, and he could see it was me but all he could do was shout, 'Holly, Holly!' in despair as he saw me ring off . . .

In fact, the truth didn't occur to me until biology. He was ending it. He was ending it because I hadn't seen him this weekend and I hadn't liked the ear-kissing. Why hadn't I realised sooner? It all fitted. All my bubbles of hope popped. I could barely manage to do quarter-hearted (i.e. less than half-hearted) work. In fact, only the fear of getting into trouble stopped me from texting him on silent when Mrs Shah was writing on the board in biology.

Every minute was agony, thinking about bumping into him at some point and him saying, 'Holly – get the message, I don't like you any more.' I couldn't believe it was all over, already. So soon! We hadn't even gone up to London together or anything!

Back home I hid under my duvet, paralysed with misery. What if you only got a share of good days per year, and I had used them all up in one go, and it was all bad from now on?

Finally, I emerged from the duvet and got into my wardrobe to call Poppy. She wasn't stroppy or anything, thank God. She said sympathetically that Luke was out. I had just picked up my phone to try Luke again, when it rang!

Calling: Turd-face

It took me a few seconds of bafflement to realise it was Claudia! Changing her name in my mobile to 'something more accurate' had been Poppy's idea: she had put it on my phone a while ago, during a sleepover.

If anything, realising it was Claudia made my baffledness increase.

'Hello?' I said hesitantly.

It was all very surreal. I was sat in my wardrobe, as if this was a perfectly normal phone call, but actually it was Claudia. Turd-face.

'You seemed a bit . . . odd today at school. I was worried about you. Is everything OK?'

If I hadn't already been sitting down, I would have fallen over in shock. I opened and closed my mouth a few times.

'Holly?'

I thought she might as well hear about it from me, so she could sneer about it. So I said, 'It's Luke.' In a small, defensive voice.

My voice was small and defensive. It was humiliating to admit, after my confidence at our sleepover. But she was going to find out anyway.

But Claudia didn't seem to be sneering.

'I thought it might be,' she said sympathetically. 'What happened?'

To be honest, I needed to make sense of it all, so I told her what had happened. Only the short, fifteen-minute version, though. I wasn't sure about confiding in Claudia. Surely she would use whatever I said against me?

But Claudia listened and said maybe it had all just been a mistake, even though it clearly hadn't.

'Have you tried calling him?'

'His phone is off.'

'Get Poppy to ask him if he's OK.'

'I did. He's out.'

'You'll see him on Saturday,' she said, as if a) it were true, and b) I could possibly wait until then.

'I won't,' I said. 'I got it wrong. I forgot he had another film club on Saturday.'

I was really annoyed with myself but I started crying, I couldn't help it. Claudia was actually sweet, for a monster, and said not to worry. Just before she said goodbye, she suggested I should go round there just in case, so I walked up the road in order to post a pretend letter (the Royal Mail are going to receive an envelope with no address and no stamp), but Luke's light was indeed out. I stood outside the Taylors' house for a minute and realised it was getting really cold in the evenings. Something in the air made me realise it would be Christmas soon, although we hadn't even had Fireworks Night yet. Suddenly the sight of Luke's bedroom window, dark and unilluminated, filled me with a kind of hollow despair, and I had to go back home.

OK, Holly. It was over. That's all there was to it. I had to get on with my life:

Reasons to Keep Living

1. *This is really no problem for my life. All I have to do is simply go back to how things were before Luke.*

2. *I can focus solely on my GCSEs and do brilliantly, especially on 'To Kill a Mockingbird.'*

3. *I can be a really, really brilliant friend to everyone and just help them with their own love lives.*

4. *I can tidy my room and really enjoy being in it and knowing where everything is.*

5. *I can be nicer to Jamie (who can't help being annoying because he is only eleven).*

On Tuesday evening when I got home, Dad asked if I was OK and I pretended I was stressed about school. The truth was that I had saved up all my miserableness for when I got home. I had to pretend to be OK at school because there was no way I was going to cry in lessons! Nothing was that bad. Actually, Claudia was still being really nice at school. And it was funny – Poppy seemed almost bothered about Claudia being so nice to me!

I collapsed on my bed like a purple and grey-uniformed blob of misery. Then I had to get up again and actually climb under the duvet, because Mum had refused to put the heating on, claiming it wasn't winter yet, even though it clearly was.

Suddenly, it happened. Luke phoned my mobile from his land-line!

It was unbelievable.

'How are you?' he said, sounding all normal, as if nothing had changed.

'Look,' I said shakily as I got up from under the duvet and climbed into the wardrobe, determined to be brave, 'we might as well get it over with.'

'What?'

How could he pretend to be confused, when he had started all this?

'I mean, it's your decision. I'm sorry the ear-kissing tickles, but it does, OK? And I didn't see you at the weekend because I thought I needed to see Poppy. And, if you want to break up, just say. Don't ignore me.'

'What are you talking about?'

Did he think I was stupid?

'You blanked me!'

'When?'

'On the bus. Early yesterday morning.'

'You weren't on my bus yesterday morning.'

'No – I missed your bus. But I saw you in the window, and I waved, and you didn't smile or anything. And then you turned your phone off!'

'No,' said Luke slowly, 'the bus was just going really fast. I did smile. You probably just didn't see me in time.'

Oh.

'What about your phone?' I said in a slightly smaller voice.

'Oh, it's out of battery,' said Luke. I heard rummaging in the background. 'My charger's a bit temperamental. There's a wire hanging out the back so I kind of have to hold it – right, I'm just charging it now. Listen, do you want to go to London on Friday night? I haven't seen you for ages!'

Hurrah!

Then he said, 'Holly, why do I have about ten missed calls from you?'

Urk. Think quickly.

'Oh – my phone must have unlocked itself in my bag and hit redial,' I said, as I banged my head against the inside of the wardrobe.

Thank goodness for that.

As he rang off, Ivy came in. We were getting on a lot better than we used to. We'd been forced into talking more whenever she came back from uni, because her exercise bike and rowing machine were plonked in my room. I think Mum's original idea had been that I would do some exercise, but I just used them as clothes stands.

Ivy saw me sat there in the wardrobe and announced in a news-headline type voice, 'Girl Hits Problem *En Route* to Narnia.'

I explained about the noise insulation the wardrobe provided against eavesdropping.

'That's a brilliant idea,' Ivy said, staring at the wardrobe looking awed. 'I wish I'd thought of that.'

Which was a bit of a weird thing to say, because Ivy didn't have anything to hide, did she?

Ivy sighed heavily as she got onto the exercise bike, which is what I do when I want someone to ask what's wrong. (I mean sighing, not getting on the exercise bike. That would mean something *majorly* wrong.)

'What's up?' I asked obligingly.

Ivy sighed. 'Nothing.'

'Are you sure?'

She looked at me and admitted, 'OK. It's my uni course, that's all. Some of the science and stuff is really hard.'

Oh! So that's what her long face had been all about! She wasn't homesick, she was stressed.

I didn't want to say, 'Well, it *is* a degree in Sports Science.' It was no secret that Ivy had failed her A-levels and only just managed to get into university. And I was sure work was really hard at degree level.

Ivy continued, 'I kind of went into it for the practical part, you know? I want to be a coach, not a science teacher.'

I didn't know what to say, but then I remembered that the most reassuring thing was empathy, so I said, 'I know how you feel. I said "I ate the house at five past four" by mistake in German the other day.'

But Ivy just sighed again.

I was about to say more supportive things when my phone rang!

'I'll go,' mouthed Ivy and headed out the door.

It was Claudia!

I told her the good news about Luke, wondering if she might sound a bit annoyed that I was happy again. However, Claudia sounded pleased. 'That's brilliant,' she said, continuing, 'I mean, it was all you needed, wasn't it, with that whole thing with Poppy! It must have been additional stress for you.'

What whole thing with Poppy? What was stressful for me?

She continued, 'It's not the ideal time for her to be getting annoyed.'

'Hmm,' I said slowly, trying to sound really neutral so she would just keep talking. Claudia clearly thought that I already knew, whatever it was. Amazingly, my strategy worked.

'Honestly Holly, I know what she's like,' she confided. 'I wouldn't worry about it. It will blow over eventually. She's just ridiculously temperamental. I've been there, remember? I mean, you just wouldn't neglect her for Luke, the whole thing is ridiculous. She's just . . . you know, having a momentary strop.'

What? Poppy had said to my face that she was OK. But actually she was saying stuff behind my back? And talking about it with Claudia?

'She'll be OK,' Claudia said soothingly. 'I'm sure. Try not to worry. I'll try to smooth things over.'

'That would be good,' I said slowly, my stomach lurching.

So we talked a bit more and Claudia said we should support each other and she'd see me tomorrow!

I sat in the same place staring at my phone for quite a while after we'd finished talking. Then I carefully changed 'Turd-face' back to 'Claudia'.

I had really thought I had made an enemy. But why would Claudia point me in the right direction with Poppy, apart from that she genuinely wanted to help me? If she had wanted things to get worse between Poppy and me, she would have just let the situation continue, without warning me, wouldn't she?

London Calling

School was really getting in the way of my life as girlfriend and rebel. Honestly, teachers were just giving us so much work! German ... essays for Extra English ... non-Luke-related maths ... they seemed to think that we didn't have lives as well as school! I complained to Sasha and she said, 'Just do a bit of it.'

'What?'

'You're too academic.'

She was so brave. She thought it was fine to turn up at school with things half done, or missing altogether. If I so much as forgot my science goggles, I practically had a heart attack.

Apart from that, though, things were OK. Claudia and I appeared to be on the same side again, and Luke was even taking me to London after school on Friday night!

Although, I did feel a bit defensive around Poppy after what Claudia had said.

'Are you going to say you're at my house?' said Poppy, when I told her about Friday. She seemed a bit weary for some reason. She added 'Don't you have Extra English?'

What, now she was lecturing me about Extra English when actually she was feeling annoyed about being neglected?

'Well, it's optional, isn't it? I haven't seen Luke for ages!'

How cool. I was not strictly supposed to go up to London without a grown-up, so it had an exciting air about it. We would probably get to see some famous people, as well!

'It's not like you to miss school stuff,' said Poppy.

Why did she sound so shocked?

'But I can't wait until next weekend to see Luke. I've only just got things back on track with him! I have to do something.'

'I thought you were going to tell your mum about him?'

I thought about it. 'No, it's not a good time, not after the past week. I really need everything to be simple for a little while.'

'OK,' said Poppy. She went a bit quiet. Then she added, 'But this isn't simple – it's getting quite complicated.'

That was all very well, but she wasn't in my shoes. What other choice did I have?

Why are parents only observant when you don't want them to be? Friday at breakfast I casually mentioned that I would be going to Poppy's that evening and Mum said, 'Don't you have Extra English tonight?'

What? She never, ever paid attention to what I did academically! (Only sporting achievements counted to my mum.)

Should I say I had forgotten? Or that a fox had appeared and eaten Mrs Mitford's notes, or . . . I looked at my toast.

Finally I improvised, 'It's been cancelled this week.'

'Why?'

'Rainy weather,' I said, inspired.

'How come?'

Actually, maybe that wasn't a very good excuse. It was good for PE. But possibly less suitable for English?

'Er – the classroom got a leak,' I said, because I could hardly think of something different now. 'The guttering, er, broke, and all the water was coming in through the wall.'

'But there must be tons of other rooms free, after school?'

Oh *God*.

'This one has got the projector screen in it.'

'And you need that for English?'

'Yes.'

'Right,' said Mum, looking at me strangely. Could she tell I was lying? Panic! Panic!

But she just said, 'Oh well, have a good time at Poppy's. Honestly, you two are inseparable these days.'

Little did she know.

Luke and I didn't see any celebrities in Leicester Square, just one person who looked like someone from TV but it wasn't actually them. We couldn't afford to go on any of the arcade games in the Trocadero Centre, so we raced coins down the sides of the escalators instead. It was so cool. Then, after I'd made us test some of the perfumes and aftershaves in The Body Shop, we got a Burger King and ate it in the little park in the square. Luke threw some chips at the pigeons, which was really funny.

On the way home, he announced, 'I'll walk you home.'

'You can't!' I said in alarm.

'No,' he said seriously, 'I will. Right up to the door, then give you a big snog in front of everyone in your family.'

'Ha ha, very funny.'

In the end we ran really quietly past my house, so I wouldn't be seen, and went back to his house. We were the only ones in!

'Come upstairs,' he said, 'I want to show you this cool film trailer I downloaded on my computer.'

I hesitated and he said, 'Film – trailer – problem – where?'

'Nothing,' I replied.

So, without discussing it further or anything, we went into his room! It had an undertone of thrillingness to it. I mean, I had been alone with him before, but not in his bedroom.

Luke's room was funny: it was really tidy and smelled of boy, kind of like Lynx aftershave mixed with old trainers.

'Oh, you've put new film posters up in here!' I said in surprise as I stepped through the door, just as Luke said, 'Ta daaa! This is my room!'

I hoped he might not have been listening to me, but he stopped short and said, 'What do you mean, new posters? Have you been in here before?'

I gulped and plonked myself onto his stripey duvet, looking down at my shoes. 'Well, last summer, Poppy got the key to your room and we came in here for like, five seconds. We looked at your DVDs, that's all.'

Thank Goodness I realised Luke was laughing. 'I thought she came in here. She's rubbish. She moves stuff!'

I could have fainted with relief.

'She thinks the spare key is this big secret, but it's not very subtle when my stuff turns up in her room.'

Then he started tickling me, saying, 'But I didn't know she had invited you in! That was my job!'

I realised that I was flat on the bed and Luke was effectively on top of me which was quite interesting, but I stopped and said, 'I should go.' Not because I didn't want to see where things might go, but because I did – and it was better avoided, since I did actually want to focus on my GCSEs and stuff.

'Hang on, my mum gave me your ticket for the firework display,' said Luke.

As he handed it to me and I said thank you, my phone started ringing. It was Claudia.

'You said you were free tomorrow night, after all?' Claudia said. 'Come over for the yoga. I'm inviting Poppy too.'

'OK – cool!' I said, pleased. She didn't need to have done that, did she? Poppy had always been a bit hard on Claudia.

I had just hung up when the phone rang again.

It was Mum!

My stomach lurched. Oh God, she had found out Luke and I had been together, and –

'Why is it ten p.m.?' said Mum. She was speaking quickly, because she thinks mobile calls are really expensive. (Jo says her mum is the same and just says things like 'Dinner's at six! OK, bye,' then hangs up.)

It was a bit of a random question. Why was it ten p.m.? You

might as well ask, why is green green?

'I thought you'd be back by now,' she added.

Oh.

'I'm still at Poppy's,' I said (not bad, truthful apart from the 'still').

Luke raised his eyebrows.

'I expect you've been sat around watching films?' Mum said accusingly.

For a moment I felt like telling her that my evening had involved all kinds of exercise – walking (around Leicester Square), precision throwing (chips at pigeon) and even tickling (on Luke's bed).

I seriously considered it. I even opened my mouth.

But then I thought, no, how would she react? It would mean major stress and unpleasantness. Major. So I took the easy route.

'I'll be home in five minutes.'

Uptown Girl

It was so lovely sleeping in on Saturday. Not having to set my alarm for school – hurrah! Not dragging myself out of bed in the cold and dark – hurrah! Although Ivy came in to use the exercise bike at about midday so I had to wake up, at least.

'Aren't you working on your coursework today?' I asked, as I pulled on my bathrobe and looked through a pile of library books for something to read.

Ivy pulled a face. Were things still going badly?

'You know what happened last week?' she said, clearly wanting to talk about it. 'I failed another written module! I'm doing really well in the practical stuff. But this was assessed coursework. If I fail this semester, I'm not allowed to be on extra-curricular teams. And I'm the best karate student they've had for years!'

I didn't know what to say. But she didn't cry or anything, she just started cycling really fast. So I went downstairs and made us both some tea.

It was the first time I had been to Claudia's house. She lived in Lansdowne, the posh bit of town. My dad dropped us off because he was heading that way to play golf, and even agreed to pick us up again later.

Luke had called earlier and said, 'Do you want to come round the park with me and Craig after film club tonight? He's going to show me some karate kicks.'

'I can't,' I had said. 'I'm seeing Claudia. Poppy and I are doing a yoga DVD at her house.'

I heard what sounded like Luke dropping his phone in shock.

'What, Poo-brains?' he said, retrieving his phone.

'Turd-face,' I corrected automatically, relieved that it wasn't the idea of me doing yoga that had sent him into shock. Then I said, 'No, listen. I like her again now. She's being really nice.'

He said doubtfully, 'Well, it's good that everyone's getting on. That's what you said before, isn't it?'

'Exactly,' I said. Claudia was an ally. I needed her.

So, I took along my DVD of *Bend it Like Beckham* for Claudia to borrow because, even though it was really old, she'd said she still hadn't seen it.

It was so cool. We had Claudia's house to ourselves! Enviously, I imagined the freedom of my mum being away – no eavesdropping, no restrictions . . . This was the first time in ages when I had been able to tell the truth about where I was going. My mum was such hard work!

'Auntie Maria's gone to London tonight,' explained Claudia as she nonchalantly showed Poppy and me into a vast living room with white leather sofas and a huge TV screen at one end.

Claudia was acting as if this was a totally normal living room. Personally I felt like jumping up and down on a leather sofa and shouting, 'Wow!' But I decided that resisting would look more sophisticated.

'It's nice and warm in here,' I said. I had asked Mum again if we could have the heating on and she had again refused. Apparently the fact that there was Christmas stuff already in the shops didn't mean it was winter, and it was perfectly normal to have to wear three scarves in bed.

Claudia curled up on one of the sofas, kicking off her fluffy slippers. 'There's underfloor heating,' she said matter-of-factly.

I sat down on another sofa. There was a low table next to me bearing a lamp with a beautiful, pleated, white silk shade. A chunky silver photo frame below held four different shots of Claudia's mum with her boyfriend in what looked like Venice. Vanessa Sheringham was very distinctive-looking, with the same penchant for heavy eye make-up as Claudia.

'Shall we cook some food before we watch the film?' said Poppy.

'I'll get us a takeaway,' said Claudia.

Cool! Getting a takeaway was a real treat.

But Claudia seemed almost apologetic about it! 'Sorry,' she continued, 'there's not much stuff we could cook. She's not one of those mums who buys stuff like that – I mean, even when she's here.'

'Don't worry!' said Poppy.

Claudia's Auntie Maria had left out some grocery money and

we worked out we could actually afford to get one of those deals where you get an extra-large pizza with cheesy crust, a big bottle of fizzy drink, chicken wings, garlic bread and ice cream! The delivery man was clearly impressed. Then we watched film trailers on Sky while we ate, happily ignoring the yoga DVD.

Soon I was too full from the pizza to speak but Poppy managed, 'God, all these trailers are for love stories!'

'Who was that guy outside HMV with you that time?' said Claudia. 'You should get together with him!'

Poppy looked puzzled.

Claudia added, 'Although, you might want to improve his dress sense.'

'Oh – you mean Craig,' I said. 'No, that was his uniform. He's doing work experience at HMV, for film studies. Luke is gutted, he wanted to do a placement as well but they only had a few spaces.'

'What, DVD-straightening?' said Claudia.

'Exactly! Invaluable experience!' I giggled.

Poppy laughed. She got up to go to the bathroom, before coming back in and hesitating.

'Under the stairs,' said Claudia, probably used to this.

'Too many doors,' I said as Poppy left the room. 'You should label the bathroom!'

When Poppy had gone, Claudia gave me a supportive smile.

'Don't worry,' she said, strangely.

'What do you mean?'

'Well, she's just a bit jealous, isn't she? I'll talk to her for you if you want.'

'Jealous?'

'Of you having a boyfriend.'

That was a bit weird.

'Really?' I said.

'A bit, yes. I mean, she just made that comment about love stories, didn't she? That was clearly a bit of a dig at you.'

Was it?

'Has Poppy said to you that she's jealous?'

'Well, to be honest, yes' said Claudia. 'A few times.'

Blimey.

'That seems a bit babyish,' I said, confused.

'Well, that's just what she told me,' said Claudia, adding in a soothing tone, 'That's partly why I invited you tonight. You know, I thought it might help you both sort it out.'

'No – sorry – thank you.'

The idea of Poppy complaining about me made me so angry that when she came back into the room I could barely look at her! In fact, Claudia's support had the opposite effect to that she intended. I mean, Poppy was acting like a child. And I was really hurt that she was talking about it behind my back to Claudia. We were the ones who were best friends: couldn't she have said something to me directly instead of keeping secrets?

'What?' said Poppy a bit defensively, noticing my expression.

I would just confront her now. I hated conflicts but this needed sorting out. After all, Claudia was there, she would be on my side.

I had just opened my mouth when Claudia looked at us both and jumped in, rather randomly, with, 'Holly, is your mum still being weird?'

What?

'You know. About boys.'

Poppy laughed, presumably because of course my mum was still being weird.

I didn't laugh along with Poppy. I didn't want her laughing as if things were normal, when actually she was being such a cow behind my back. Poppy looked at me quizzically, as if to ask what was wrong. I just looked away.

'I don't think my mum is going to change any time soon,' I told Claudia.

Claudia paused thoughtfully, then said, 'Is it just your mum who is strict, or your dad too?'

'Just her, really. I mean, Dad always backs her up. But she's the one who makes the fuss.'

'It's weird,' said Claudia pensively. 'I mean, most parents aren't like that. Not that mine are ever in the same room. I was just wondering if . . .'

Then, uncharacteristically, she went quiet.

'What?'

'Nothing,' said Claudia, looking quickly at me then looking away again. 'It's just, well, I was wondering whether she had some personal reason for being so anti-men. Did you say your mum gets particularly uptight if anyone mentions, like, getting pregnant?'

'God, yes, once there was this one storyline on *EastEnders* – what do you mean?'

'Just wondering. You know, maybe she, like, had an affair or something.'

I laughed, but Claudia appeared to be warming to her theme. 'Yes – a passionate affair resulting in an unwanted child . . . and she is scared you will make the same mistake that she did!'

She was mad. Totally mad. I was still laughing, when Claudia said, 'And it is, like, an ongoing tension trying to hide the truth.' She paused then spoke really slowly, as if she was working something out in her head, 'Because, no matter how hard she tries to make them change, this unwanted child is not like the rest of the family.'

Poppy and Claudia both looked at me.

Then Poppy said, 'Holly, she is always trying to get you to be sporty.'

It's at moments like this in books when people start hyperventilating. I might have done it too, if only I knew what hyperventilating actually was.

I managed, 'But it doesn't make any sense. I've got brown hair like my dad. I look like both my mum and my dad.'

Poppy said, 'But it's not impossible.'

What, so even Poppy thought it sounded accurate?

I excused myself and sat in Claudia's downstairs loo to chill out. It was a ridiculous theory. Ridiculous. Just because I was a bit different didn't mean I didn't belong, did it?

However, when I went back in, Poppy and Claudia's sympathetic faces filled me with sudden doubt. Could it possibly be true? What if my mum had had an affair and I was not my dad's?

Claudia was really nice and supportive. She told me about a friend of a friend who had found out the same thing and it had all worked out fine in the end, once they had all got through the ensuing divorce and the move to a whole new part of the country in order to heal the emotional scars.

Instead of doing the yoga DVD, Claudia kindly put on *Bend it Like Beckham* to distract me, but instead of following the heroine's desire to play in a girls' football team, I just sat there, worried. It was the same on the journey home, when Dad picked me up. Poppy stayed over at Claudia's in the end but I wanted to go home to sort my head out. I was suddenly looking at my Dad differently, trying to work out if we really looked similar or whether I had been mistaken all these years. You know, we had a similar sort of nose and the same sort of complexion, but there were differences too. He was tall, whereas I was short. He had grey hair, while mine was light brown. He'd never had braces on his teeth. Could it really be a possibility that to my mum, I was just a constant reminder of her previous indiscretion? No wonder I didn't fit in!

Don't Speak

'She's being a bitch,' said Ivy. It was Sunday and she was on the phone from uni, where she was preparing for a witches-and-wizards-themed party. I couldn't believe that the one time I needed Ivy at home, to discuss my illicit parentage, she wasn't around. What with everything going on, I had forgotten it was Halloween this weekend. Halloween had been somewhat eclipsed by Fireworks Night, since it didn't present any obvious romantic opportunities (although, covering myself with a ghost-style sheet would have been a great way to conceal braces/tangly hair). I wish someone had told Jamie, Asif and Imran that when asked 'Trick or Treat?' that it was not acceptable to say, 'Treat please.' A gang of five-year-olds put silly string ALL OVER the front of our house.

'Look, Holly,' Ivy continued, 'Claudia's mum might have had affairs, but it doesn't mean ours did. Claudia watches too many soap operas.'

'Her mum's *in* a soap opera.'

'Well, there you go. Born drama queen.'

'But what if she's right? And I was looking at Dad last night in the car. There are some things that are really quite different, you know.'

'Please tell me this is not what you said earlier.'

'Well, it's true.'

'Holly, Dad being taller and having grey hair is not cause for concern. It is quite normal, you know. But if you're really worried about it, just ask Mum.'

When Mum got back from the supermarket, I went and helped her with the bags.

'Can you put that bag in the fridge?' she said, bending over to extract things from the car boot. She looked back to see me hesitating, and said, 'It's got yoghurts in.'

'Is my dad really my dad?' I said.

I thought everything would go sort of slow motion and meaningful like in a film, i.e. Mum's shoulders would tense significantly, then she would act in some evasive manner that would immediately indicate I had guessed the long-buried truth. Instead she gave me a funny look and went, 'Of course he is, Holly, don't be ridiculous. Can you take those eggs too? But be careful.'

Confused, I picked up both bags and went into the house to put everything in the fridge, then went back outside.

'So, if you didn't have an affair, how come I'm not sporty and you all are?'

Mum laughed at my face and said, 'Holly, honestly. I think you read too much.'

Oh yes, that was the problem. Me reading.

'It's all that stuff from the library with the bright covers. If you got out more in the fresh air, you would never have such melo-dramatic ideas. And you would enjoy exercise, if only you would try.'

I made a face, but I guessed that was good, then. There was no sinister reason behind me not fitting in. The only reason was, well, myself.

'Any more bizarre questions?' Mum said. 'Or can I unpack the potatoes?'

Because of Extra English I didn't get to talk to Poppy alone until the bus journey home on Monday. Well, I say *talk*. Actually we had another one of those uneasy silences. I was just wondering whether it was an OK silence or not, when Poppy burst out, 'And another thing.'

Which was a strange thing to start a conversation with, sug-gesting she'd already been having an internal argument with me for some time.

Why was Poppy annoyed with me? What had I done? If any-thing, she should have been apologising to me, for talking to Claudia about me behind my back!

Poppy continued, 'You told Luke I went into his room!'

Oh God. Honestly. One minute my life was normal and I was complaining about how boring it was, and the next it was like something out of one of those American TV series, but without the good bits like being in California and being really rich and gorgeous.

'Did Luke mention it?'

She nodded frostily.

Did Luke have to be quite so honest and straightforward all the time? Couldn't he lie, just a little bit? It would make life so much easier.

'He wasn't annoyed with you, was he?' I ventured. 'He thought it was funny!'

'That's not the point. You're telling him stuff that was secret! Between us!'

No I wasn't! Where on earth had she got a weird idea like that from?

'It wasn't like that at all! And if you'd give me a chance to explain . . . the whole thing was an accident. He caught me out. You know I am a rubbish liar.'

Poppy gave me a funny look. 'Forget it,' she said, and looked out of the window again. She was paying more attention to the scenery on this bus ride than in all the time I had known her.

We'd never really argued before, not like this. I felt all shaky with adrenalin. I didn't know what to say. So I just pretended to look at my phone. (How did people act unperturbed before mobile phones were invented?) All this just went to show that Claudia was right: Poppy was judgemental, temperamental and stubborn. I hadn't noticed because, until now, only Claudia had been on the receiving end.

On Wednesday night I didn't notice my phone beeping, but then I saw the light on and realised I had missed a call from Luke! I phoned him back and he said, 'We're going out, meet me at the end of the road!'

'"We" as in "you and me and Craig"?'

'No! You and me!'

'It's a weekday evening!'

'I know, but it's a surprise!'

He sounded so excited. I couldn't exactly disappoint him by saying no. It was all very romantic and daring and spontaneous! My evening *had* been lined up as follows:

- *Eating the other half of the Flake I had managed to save from the weekend by wrapping it in sellotape and hiding it from myself in my sock drawer.*
- *Doing my essay for Extra English.*

Now it was:

- *Snogging Luke in mystery location.*

Except I wasn't sure how to get out of the house. And I didn't have much time. But I got ready anyway then called out that I was going to Poppy's to do my homework just as I was leaving. So Mum didn't see I had lots of make-up on! It didn't seem like a very good idea to call Poppy and tell her, considering our fight on Monday and what Claudia had told me about her being jealous. She would think I was just rubbing it in.

'Are you OK?' asked Luke when I met him at the end of the street.

'Fine,' I claimed. I really wanted to talk to him about Poppy.

But I couldn't exactly discuss it, because, after all, she was his sister! It would have felt weird.

The surprise was really cool. The local cinema was screening an old Luc Besson film. We turned up just as it was starting, so afterwards Luke said, 'We missed out on ice cream. Let's share some on the way home.'

The lady at the counter seemed a bit baffled that we were buying ice cream on our way home, but she said there weren't any rules about it, and it was our decision.

But then, out of nowhere, the evening went wrong!

Basically, all that happened was that Luke picked up two tubs of ice cream and said, 'Which shall we get, strawberry or lemon cheesecake?'

'I don't mind,' I said, because I didn't mind.

'Choose one, though.'

'You choose.'

'But I asked you.'

'But I like them both, so we should get whatever is your favourite.'

He didn't say anything, just looked at the ice cream then looked at me again.

I was being really nice and obliging, i.e. I wanted to have the one that he wanted the most. So I said again, 'I really don't mind!'

But he seemed to not be very pleased and said, 'Oh forget it,' picked up a weird coconut one that I definitely didn't like and went to the till with that.

God, boys were strange. It was mad. There were some things that I absolutely loved (snogging, intellectual conversations, the togetherness), and some things which were a right pain (Craig, ear-snogging). And, now, making joint decisions.

We headed back to the house in silence with the coconut ice cream, instead of sharing it and giggling together, while I thought about how quickly things had plummeted into awfulness. How was I going to tell people tomorrow that Luke had broken up with me because I didn't mind about what ice cream we ate? I didn't know what I'd done wrong. I had never had an argument like that with any of my girl friends! It was really confusing.

Blinking back tears, I suddenly felt the desire to get back home.

Just beyond the streetlamp Luke gave me a hug goodbye, slightly stiffly at first, until eventually we relaxed into each other, as if touching had reminded us that we did actually like each other.

Relieved, I dashed up to the house and put my key in the lock. I swear, I did it really quietly. But then the hall light went on! My stomach lurched. Oh God, something was wrong.

'You were a bit late,' said Mum as I stepped inside. 'And your mobile was off. So I phoned Poppy's to check you were still there.'

Oh God. My worst nightmare. Why, why had I turned my phone off during the film? Wildly, I considered my options:

1. *Burst into tears and explain everything, taking care to mention that this had hardly been a night of wild rebellion involving going to third base in a red convertible: we'd just argued about ice cream.*
2. *Run away fast enough for Mum to forget she had ever seen me coming in.*

But suddenly I realised something weird: Mum was smiling. Then something even weirder happened. She walked up to me and gave me a big hug!

'Poppy told me everything!' she said.

'About what?' I managed, confused, as she released me from her grip.

'Of course you could have said something. I'm so proud of you!'

Little Lies

'You told my mum I was trying out for an all-girls' football team?' I yelled down the phone to Poppy, from inside my wardrobe. I had switched my phone back on to find a missed call from Mum and then about six from Poppy.

I looked over at my picture of Luke above my bed. How could someone that gorgeous be related to someone this stupid?

'I couldn't think of anything to say!' said Poppy. 'And we'd just watched *Bend it Like Beckham*—'

'We watched *Harry Potter* the other week, why didn't you just say I'd run off to Hogwarts?'

'Sorry – it was the best thing I could come up with at short notice. I said the film had inspired you.'

I snorted. I couldn't believe Poppy had come up with such a rubbish lie.

'Holly, you didn't warn me!' said Poppy, sounding annoyed. 'Your mum just called out of the blue, said your mobile was going through to voicemail, and asked to speak to you! I didn't know what to say! So I said you'd seen this sign at school for a football team try-out, and decided to have a go.'

The irritation and disbelief overtook me again. I turned my phone off for, like, five minutes, and this happened! 'Poppy, this is awful! She is really pleased!'

Mum had never once been proud of me before, and it was all a lie! I felt terrible!

'Well, I'm sorry. Maybe you should find someone else to lie for you,' said Poppy, sounding furious. 'Someone less babyish.'

'What?'

'That's what you said to Claudia about me, behind my back.'

'No I didn't.'

'You did. At her house.'

'I didn't!' I said. Then I remembered. 'Oh God – OK, I did say that – just one time – but I didn't mean it like that.'

I felt uneasy. Claudia knew I hadn't meant it like it sounded. She must have mentioned it and Poppy had taken it the wrong way.

'Look – I'm just saying, I would have thought of something better,' I continued. I mean, if it had been the other way round I would have, you know, kept it simple:

Simpler Excuses

- *I was in the shower because some, er – syrup went in my hair, while Poppy and I were eating home-made pancakes.*
- *I squashed a spider against my back while leaning against the wall, and fainted from the shock.*

'Why didn't you say that I was in the loo?' I said. Just once, going to the loo at a friend's house could have been useful rather than a liability.

'Holly, you've got no right to be annoyed! You should have warned me you'd said you were with me!'

OK, maybe I should have warned Poppy, but she knew what it meant if my mum called, didn't she? It felt almost as if Poppy had done this on purpose to make my life difficult. She had threatened my relationship with Luke, and now I was going to have to tell proper, major lies to Mum. Mrs Mastiff and Mum knew each other, as well. They'd met recently when Ivy was doing a summer project with Mrs Mastiff. This alone made the story so risky that I didn't even know where to start. All that, and she didn't feel any need to apologise?

I said, 'It's like you don't want to help, because you're annoyed with me about going out with Luke. It's like . . . it's like you're trying to sabotage it.'

'Why on earth would I do that?'

'I don't know; you tell me,' I said. I felt sick.

'You're clearly trying to make some sort of point.'

'Well, it's just been . . . weird, hasn't it?' I would finally bring it out in the open, the stuff she had been telling Claudia, so we could sort things out properly. 'Like . . . you know . . . Luke and I have been spending lots of time together and stuff. You could just be straight with me and say something if it's a problem, instead of just getting jealous and making me feel bad, but then insisting nothing's wrong.'

'Jealous? You're saying I'm jealous?' said Poppy.

Oops. That bit had kind of slipped out. I mean, when Claudia had originally put it like that, I had been surprised, too. But it was true, wasn't it?

There was an ominous silence from Poppy's end of the phone, and then she said icily, 'Holly, that is completely out of order. You are being a complete bitch. And stop claiming that you don't like lying, when you've forced me to lie for you. For someone who claims to be all truthful, you're getting pretty good at deception.'

I couldn't believe she'd just called me a bitch. She was being so unreasonable!

With that, I did something I had never done before in the whole history of my friendship with Poppy: I hung up on her.

I felt a moment of perverse triumph. She was ruining our friendship, but I could ruin it, too. Ha! That would show her!

Then I got under my duvet and cried my eyes out.

Why Does It Aways Rain on Me?

'Let's finally get started on our netball tournament!' said Mrs Mastiff on Thursday morning, looking brightly up at the grey clouds.

It was clearly going to rain, though for a change I hoped it wouldn't, because Fireworks Night was just two days away, on Saturday night. Although, to be honest, rain was the least of my problems. It was clear that you could just do one tiny thing wrong and Poppy would really hold it against you! I couldn't believe I had been so judgemental back when Poppy wasn't speaking to Claudia. I planned to talk to Claudia during netball, because at least she would be on my side, because she had been there.

Mrs Mastiff was walking us towards the court when the first raindrops start to hit. She continued anyway, when Mrs Craignish came out from the staffroom to have a quick word with Mrs Mastiff. All I could hear was 'Health and Safety'.

'Right everyone,' announced Mrs Mastiff, visibly discontent that she wasn't allowed to torture us. 'Back inside! Into the Assembly Hall instead!'

After Mrs Craignish left, Mrs Mastiff muttered, 'It's ridiculous, you should all be outside. When I was a girl, a bit of rain never put anyone off.'

I think I may love Mrs Craignish.

Mrs Mastiff got her revenge by setting up this thing called circuit training, which is basically another term for hell. It involved the horse (this old, dusty thing you have to vault over), skipping ropes, and dumb-bells. I was actually beginning to miss netball.

I failed to catch Claudia's eye during the lesson, although I tried a few times.

So I talked to Sasha, who was by me in the queue for vaulting.

'I'm tired,' I told her, as we approached the front of the line. 'I didn't sleep very well. Luke fell on me during the night.'

'Oh my God, Holly! When—'

'No, not Luke himself, the drawing stuck above my bed.'

I looked at the vaulting thing, a few metres away. According to Mrs Mastiff and everyone else in my class, I was supposed to run at it, then leap over it in some sort of elegant manner.

'Think of it as a barrier between you and going home,' said Sasha encouragingly.

I hesitated.

'OK, seeing Luke then.'

I took a deep breath and ran at it, only to have the usual thing happen. First I sort of tried to jump onto it but actually just ran into it, banging my toe. Then I tried to climb over and ended up marooned on top of it, before eventually rolling over and falling off the other side.

After PE, rubbing my bruises, I limped over to Claudia's locker.

'How's it going?' I asked Claudia.

'Fine,' she said as she brushed her dark hair.

'Did you hear about what happened with me and Poppy?'

'Yes,' said Claudia. It was strange. That was all she said. In fact, she sounded more thoughtful and uneasy than outraged on my behalf!

'I totally know what you mean now,' I said, trying again.

'About . . .'

'About Poppy being temperamental! You know, being a bit jealous and stuff.'

'OK,' said Claudia, looking around, 'but I'm not really very comfortable saying things like that behind Poppy's back.'

Er – what?

'But you're the one who said that, originally!'

Claudia paused from brushing her hair, then said thoughtfully, 'I feel I should support Poppy and respect her opinion and stuff. I'm being there for her when she's upset, that's all.'

What? WHAT?

'What are you saying, exactly?'

'I'm saying, I'm not really involved in this.'

Not involved?

'Are you telling me that you're siding with her?' I said, in outrage. This was cheating! I wasn't sure how, but it was. It shouldn't be allowed! 'I supported you when things were difficult! All that time! And now you're refusing to support me back?'

'But you were never actually much help, were you?' said Claudia.

'You said—'

'Be honest. You liked things just the way they were, with everyone thinking you were so nice. Holly and Poppy. Holly and Luke. It suited you that I wasn't around because you could keep everything for yourself.'

I was stunned. 'That's not true. I tried really hard to sort things out! Poppy was just angry with you for going off with Jez!'

I couldn't believe Claudia really had blamed me for their conflict. Jo had been right. And all this when Claudia was the one who had messed up that friendship, not me!

'That's rubbish,' I managed. 'And you're twisting things if you think that I stole Poppy away from you. You can't steal people. They have to want to go.'

'Maybe you should listen to yourself,' Claudia replied simply. 'Maybe your friendship with Poppy has just, you know, run its course.'

'Are you saying this fight is permanent?' I said, shocked into responding. Surely this was mendable?

Claudia shrugged. 'Sorry Holly,' she said, 'but friendships don't last forever, do they? Nothing does.'

Ain't No Sunshine

It had never crossed my mind that friendships didn't last. Ever since the first day of school I had been wandering about, content with my existing friends, and it turned out that all that time I should have been cultivating some sort of back-up group!

That afternoon during art I gave myself a stern talking-to about being a Cool Person who didn't need specific friends, because everyone was lovely and would just let me join their groups. But who would I be friends with now? I looked around the art room. Jo, Charlotte and Bethan were likely to remain neutral, which was all very well when you were Switzerland in World War Two but not very useful in a Year Ten situation. Then there were the Squares headed up by Susanna Forbes, but I just couldn't imagine what we could talk about together, me not speaking Latin or anything. And I blatantly had nothing in common with the sporty crowd, although they were all very well in a rosy-cheeked, over-enthusiastic kind of way.

Anyway, my first mission when I finally got home was some

damage limitation. I found Mum and Dad together in the living room. Dad was putting on his trainers and a foolish woolly hat, presumably to go for a run. Mum was finishing restringing her badminton racquet. It certainly didn't look like Mum was hiding a guilty secret from Dad. But then, I was lying to her. Maybe she was keeping stuff from me, as well.

'I didn't make the football team,' I told Mum.

She put down the racquet. 'Oh no!'

'Mrs Mastiff was pleased I tried,' I improvised. Before she could say anything more, I turned and went back upstairs, annoyed with Poppy. She had made me lie. Direct, proper lies. And Mum had sounded like she cared, although she wasn't usually at all bothered about my school stuff! She was actually interested for once, and it was all deceit!

I decided to lie on my bed with my hair over my face, as befitted my tragic life.

All-purpose Sources of Comfort for Whatever Has Just Happened

- *I am much more grown up than everybody else involved.*
- *Everyone is going to die at some point anyway so it doesn't matter.**

Suddenly I had to move my hair off my face, because my mobile was ringing.

'Meet me in the park,' said Luke.

* Slightly less comforting point of view.

When I heard Mum go out to badminton I just went out, closing the door quietly so Dad or Jamie wouldn't hear.

Luke and I sat together on the park bench in the freezing cold and Luke gave me a surprise present: the DVD of the film we'd seen! I was thrilled that everything was definitely OK again after our ice cream argument.

'I just wanted to say thank you,' said Luke. He gave me a big hug.

'For what?'

'For giving Claudia the idea.'

'What idea?'

'It's so cool. Didn't she tell you?'

Clearly it was best to just stay quiet until he told me whatever it was that I already knew.

'Claudia says she can arrange work experience for me where her mum works! You know, at the TV studio! Isn't that amazing? It will be, you know, behind the scenes, and she can show me around. It will be so cool!'

'Did Claudia call you?' I said lightly, my head working overtime. Luke was fizzing with excitement, anyone could see that.

'She phoned for Poppy last night and I answered.'

I suddenly felt sick. Really sick. I couldn't help it. Could Claudia be after Luke? She had been, momentarily. But that was ages ago, wasn't it?

Luke continued burbling away about the work experience. I managed to smile and say, 'That's great,' but either my smile or my voice conflicted with my words, because Luke stopped and said, 'What?'

'Nothing,' I said valiantly.

It was exactly like in this old film called *Dangerous Liaisons*. Exactly.

Well, almost.

There's a bit when the female lead character talks about training herself not to show emotion. As a young girl she would stick a fork into her hand under the dining table and conceal the pain. The trouble was, I had spent my childhood just eating my dinner, like I was supposed to. Which probably explained why now I was no good at pretending.

'Really?' said Luke.

'I'm fine.' I didn't know whether I should share my fear or not. I didn't want to seem immature.

'You look . . . underwhelmed,' said Luke cautiously. Oh no – he looked a bit deflated. I had clumsily burst his bubble.

'No, it's fine, I'm totally . . . whelmed.' I managed to continue, less feebly, 'It's great, obviously. But I thought you didn't like her?'

'You told me you liked her now.'

'Yes,' I said reluctantly.

'Was I still supposed to hate her?'

'No,' I said even more reluctantly.

'And the work experience is a brilliant idea, isn't it? She said she'd only thought of the idea because you'd mentioned it!'

I looked down and silently pulled a face at my Luc Besson DVD.

'You said on Kestrel Hill that you wanted everyone to get on,' Luke persisted.

I managed in a tiny voice, 'Things have changed.'

'I can't keep up,' said Luke.

Of course he couldn't. Girls were complicated.

'Claudia hates me,' I muttered darkly. There! I had said it.

'No, she doesn't! She was talking about you in really glowing terms.'

'What did she say?' I said suspiciously.

'She said that you were a great person, and she thought we were really good together.'

What a cow. I took a deep breath. 'Look, Poppy and I had an argument and Claudia sided with her and they aren't speaking to me.'

'What, are you five?' said Luke. He didn't say it unkindly, though.

'It feels like it sometimes. It's like a jungle!' I blinked back sudden tears. I did manage a half-laugh as I said it, since I did know it was ridiculous.

'And you're an unhappy penguin?'

I nodded.

'An unhappy penguin,' he repeated, 'lost in the jungle.'

He hugged me. I felt stupid and reassured all at once. After all, Claudia was out there somewhere in the cold, wasn't she? I was the one in Luke's arms.

Luke called me on Friday to say he was staying late at school for film studies, and why didn't we meet up after that? Personally, I was sick of hearing about film studies. I wished it had never been invented.

'What time?' I said.

'I'm not sure – I'll just knock for you.'

'You can't – my mum . . .'

'Oh yes,' he sounded irritated. 'OK, by, eight?'

I put the phone down. It was our second not-that-successful phone call this week. I had called him last night after getting home from the park. It wasn't great because he had already gone to bed, but he said sleepily that it was OK for me to talk. So I had tried to explain about Claudia, you know, about feeling so unsure that I didn't even want to go to the loo if she was there to talk about me while I was gone. But I think he thought I was mad as a balloon. So I had asked him how he felt if he argued with Craig, and Luke had yawned and said, 'We don't argue, really.' So I said, 'What would you do if you had a massive fight?' and Luke had said, 'I guess one would just punch the other and then we'd forget all about it.'

God, that sounded brilliant.

Now I lay on my bed with my hair over my face, being tragic. About five minutes later I heard footsteps on the wooden stairs leading up to my room, followed shortly after by Ivy's voice going, 'Look at you.'

It seemed that she was trying not to laugh?

'I am being the epitome of teen tragedy,' I explained, moving a chunk of hair to one side.

'Isn't it pronounced *eppy-tome*?' said Ivy.

No, it's *e-pit-ommy*. It's, like, a trick word.'

I know it's not very nice, but it was the first time in ages I felt reassured that I knew something academic. I had got a bit behind with the Extra English and Susanna kept getting really good marks, presumably with the sole intent of annoying me.

'Typical,' said Ivy, looking glum.

I sat up and swept my hair out of my face as she got on the exercise bike. 'Do you have to do that now?'

Ivy looked frustrated. 'I needed a break, sorry. I wanted to go swimming, but really I came home to work on my essay.'

Her voice sounded funny, and I realised it was stress. She was so weary of it all she could only just bring herself to squeeze out the words.

'I just keep thinking that if I have to quit all the teams, Mum will be so disappointed,' said Ivy quietly. She looked really miserable. 'You're so lucky.'

I snorted.

'No, really. You're not sporty, so she doesn't expect anything of you.'

That was one way of looking at it. No expectation meant no pressure.

'What's your essay about, anyway?'

'Biology and stuff.'

'Not pheromones?' I asked suspiciously.

Ivy shook her head, looking confused.

'Do you want me to look at it for you?' I ventured. 'I mean – I don't know if I can help, but I could try.'

Ivy brightened up. 'God, that would be great. If you don't mind? It's all in my room.'

'Look, you go swimming, I'll go and look at it.'

To be honest, I needed distracting. Big time.

Ivy had all the facts she needed in the various books and print-outs from websites scattered over her bed. They were already on her draft version, as well. The only problem seemed to be the structure – she had talked about the most interesting fact at the start, instead of starting off with an introduction. I changed things round so the different points were grouped together for and against the argument in the title. I ended up getting some scissors and physically cutting up one of the print-outs, then sellotaping it together. I left her a note explaining the main changes and went back upstairs. Sometimes, academic things were very straightforward, compared to relationships, anyway.

Stand by Me

I went round to see Luke at eight o'clock, as arranged, but Poppy who answered the door! Urk. Awkward.

'I take it you're here to see Luke?' she asked acidly.

I should have stayed at home and done a bit more of Ivy's work. Or maybe ran a small marathon. Anything would have been preferable to this.

Another voice disturbed us. 'Who's that – oh, hello Holly! I thought I heard your voice!'

Oh, great. Claudia was peering brightly around Poppy's living room door, while offering absolutely no explanation for her presence. I thought enviously of Luke and Craig simply punching each other if they ever had a massive fight. Did Claudia want Poppy's mum to adopt her or something?

'I brought your DVD with me, Holly,' Claudia continued. 'You left it at my house.'

I had expected some kind of showdown whenever I next spoke to her. But instead, seeing her reminded me with irritation that she had never shouted during our conversation last week, just been implacable and calm as if it had never occurred to her she'd betrayed me.

I said to Poppy, 'So, can I come in and wait?'

Poppy paused, just because she could, then said, 'Come in.'

The three of us filed awkwardly into the living room.

'I expect Luke will be here any minute,' I told them, looking at the time on my mobile. There was a silence again. Claudia looked from me to Poppy then back again, then said, 'I'm just going to the loo.'

Grr. I was on to her. She was after Luke. She was going to put on more perfume or get changed into something glam! But to my surprise, Claudia came back after a totally normal amount of time and, if anything, she looked a bit washed out! One point to Holly!

Then Claudia looked at me and Poppy, said, 'I'll give you two some space,' and walked back out of the room, even giving us some privacy by closing the door on her way out! Every time I thought I had Claudia figured out, she did something unexpected.

Poppy and I sat in silence in our usual seats until, unexpectedly, she picked up my DVD from the coffee table and said, 'Here, you should take this back.'

I could have apologised for our argument at that point. But she wasn't smiling at all. Why should I have to make all the effort all the time? I hadn't done anything that bad. No, she should be apologising to me. So I didn't say anything. Poppy turned the TV on and we watched in silence, until suddenly I wondered where Claudia had got to.

I hit the mute button, and Poppy obviously misunderstood and thought I was going to speak, because she took a deep breath and said, 'Look, Holly, that DVD caused more trouble than intended, OK?'

But that was when I realised I could hear a low murmur from the kitchen. A murmur of conversation.

'Yes – you're right. Can we talk in a little while?' I said, wildly. I dashed out of the front room into the kitchen where Claudia was standing talking to Luke! They were standing next to each other! Luke's schoolbag was by his feet, as if he had just got in.

'Have you been here for long?' I asked Luke, trying to conceal my shock. I noticed they were both holding half-full glasses of orange juice! Half full! No one just pours half a glass of a drink, do they? They had been here a little while!

Poppy had followed me. She said in concern, 'Claudia! Are you OK?'

Oh.

Apparently Claudia was crying. I had been so preoccupied with Luke that I hadn't noticed. Er, not to mention that minutes before, she had been fine.

Luke looked up at us with an infuriatingly concerned expression. 'She just called her mum,' he said, as if Claudia was too delicate to speak for herself.

'What's wrong?' Poppy asked Claudia.

At this Claudia blinked rapidly and all these tears fell out of her eyes, running down her cheeks. She looked endearingly vulnerable.

'My mum's staying in Italy for another week!' she said, speaking directly to Poppy, which was a bit irritating. I was putting up with all this, too. She could at least include me in the conversation, instead of indirectly implying I was no good at offering sympathy.

'I called her about coming home but she's staying!' Claudia gasped. 'And she's invited her boyfriend to visit for the extra time, but not me!'

'Won't that be because it's term-time?' I said, despite myself.

'That's what she said,' said Claudia. She started crying some more, at which Poppy and Luke both looked at me as if I had just jumped on a kitten.

Oh, for God's sake. That was hardly surprising! Was her mum just supposed to get her out of school?

'And she phoned my dad and asked him to take me out for Fireworks Night instead, as if that will cheer me up. If she really wanted me to visit her, she would have sorted it out,' said Claudia. She crumpled against Luke's shoulder, which was a bit much. What was wrong with crumpling against the fridge? Or the washing machine?

'I'm going upstairs,' I said quickly, before turning to Poppy and saying, 'I'll come and talk to you before I leave.'

With that, I ran off up to Luke's room. OK, it was a bit childish. But if I didn't remove myself from the kitchen, I was going to have to throw fridge magnets at her or something.

Luke followed me up to his room. We didn't speak until he had shut the door, but he already seemed to be able to tell that something was wrong.

'You look all tense. What's wrong?'

I looked down and traced the pattern on his duvet cover. Blue and grey stripes; proper boy colours. Either he was genuinely baffled, or really dim.

'You and Claudia,' I said finally, my voice going a bit funny. 'I arrange to meet you here, but then you don't even come into the living room and say hello. I have to go and find you with her!'

I trailed to a halt and looked at Luke for reassurance, but he seemed irritated and confused. My stomach plummeted.

'Oh my God – look, Holly, Claudia was upset, OK?'

I nodded but I could feel my mouth was set in a hard line. I couldn't seem to raise a smile. Why wasn't there some sort of textbook telling you how to deal with this stuff? Even just a worksheet would do.

'She said hello to me and I said hello back,' said Luke slowly, 'then she started crying because she'd literally just made that phone call. I couldn't exactly ignore her, could I? I suggested we go and sit with you and Poppy, but Claudia said we needed to leave you both alone together for a bit so you could make up. So that was nice of her, right?'

'But she flirted with you, once before!' I burst out.

Luke looked incredulous. 'Is that why you were upset about the work experience thing?'

I nodded.

'That was ages ago. You're being too sensitive.'

'Really?' I said, looking down again. I was upset that we were in his room and we weren't even touching each other. It felt bad.

He seemed half alarmed by my ferocity, and half irritated. 'Look, I can't win. I'm nice to her, and you think there's something going on.'

'It's not you I'm worried about, it's her,' I said.

Then he went silent, as if he was battling over what to say next. Eventually he took my hand with a sigh and said, 'Look, we're OK, aren't we?'

Phew. I smiled weakly and said lightly, 'If she went away, we would be.'

Stupidly, as it turns out. I should have said nothing at all!

Luke gave me a stern look, as if I was the horrible one, and said slowly, as if he was a teacher explaining why it was wrong to cheat in exams, 'Look. She was upset.'

Last time when I was upset about Claudia and the work experience, he had hugged me and called me a penguin. But this time something had gone wrong.

'I might go home,' I said heavily. I had that feeling. The one I knew I was going to cry but I didn't want to do it in front of anyone. I had said 'might' instead of 'will', because I hoped Luke would stop me and say, 'No! You can't go! Things are weird!'

But he didn't.

'OK,' said Luke. 'I'll see you soon, OK?'

I nodded, and paused at the door, but he had already reached for his MP3 player.

I couldn't face going to see Poppy and giving Claudia the satisfaction of seeing me upset. Instead I stumbled outside down the path, my eyes so full of tears that I didn't want to blink because they would fall out. Something had shifted with Luke, I could feel it. He hadn't offered to walk me home. He'd asked me all the other times, all of them!

And I'm sorry, but there was something funny about this whole Claudia-being-upset thing. For starters, Claudia had been absolutely fine when she had left the living room! I suppose she hadn't made that phone call yet, but did she have to be quite so upset about one phone call? And surely there were people she could go to for comfort, other than my boyfriend?'

I forced myself to slow down so I didn't reach my house too quickly. Then I called Sasha, since she was always suspicious of Claudia anyway.

'They were standing together in the kitchen and their glasses were half empty!'

'Don't be so pessimistic,' said Sasha.

'OK, half *full*.'

We went through everything that had happened. I concluded glumly. 'He actually thinks she's a human being. He said she was upset.'

'Pah!' said Sasha in disgust. In proper, friend fashion. I could always rely on Sasha. After all, none of it was my fault.

But then she said, 'But you know, though, she probably only cried on Luke because he was there.'

'But – the work experience too . . .'

'But did you mention to her that Luke wanted to do a work placement?'

'Yes. I guess so. I mentioned Luke being envious of Craig getting one.'

'Some people just need attention. And it's not like he's interested back. He's with you, isn't he?'

I nodded, which wasn't very useful over the phone; but, as I hung up and walked faster, the rhythm of my footsteps soothed me slightly. I said to myself, OK, calm down. In terms of Luke, what had actually changed? Nothing. I had a nice boyfriend who happened to be kind to other people. It wasn't actually that bad, was it, someone standing in a kitchen with someone else? In fact, things had been peaceful and fine and I had stirred it up by acting jealous for no reason, like one of those mad, possessive people.

By the time I reached my door I had calmed down. It was only when I got out my key that I noticed something unusual. The light was on and Mum was standing in the hall. And she wasn't smiling.

Rebel Rebel

'What's going on?' said Mum. I had never seen her look so angry.

'With what?' I countered, more in desperation than anything else.

'Mrs Heathfield says she saw you with a boy, walking down Rosehill Road together, the day you told me you were at football!'

Oh God. Oh God. Oh God.

'It was Poppy said I was at football, not me,' I said quickly.

'Well, were you at football?'

I took a deep breath and I shook my head.

'No.'

'Well then. Who is this boy?'

I mumbled, 'It's Poppy's brother. Luke.'

'You lied to me, Holly? To sneak around with someone?'

'I'm going out with him – that's all there is to it. It's serious,' I said, suddenly angry. 'I couldn't tell you, because you're so impossible! You can't handle me having a boyfriend!'

It didn't seem fair. Not to mention that I had spent the evening on the verge of tears – hardly the heady heights of passion that she probably suspected.

'Holly Stockwell, my concern is that you're only just fifteen, and a young fifteen at that.'

Grr. She'd said that before. She didn't know a thing about my life, with the illicit trips to the recording studio and Leicester Square. I mean, that was pretty grown up, wasn't it? Someone could have offered me drugs or anything!

Mum continued, 'You're not old enough for a relationship. It could get too serious, too quickly. You need to focus.'

'What should I be focusing on?'

'Your exams,' she said firmly.

I let out a 'Pah!' noise, despite myself.

She looked surprised, so I said, 'As if you care about my exams.'

I felt so exhausted by all the tension that I started to cry. 'As if you care about anything that isn't sports, or Ivy and Jamie!'

Mum looked at me and then turned away. 'I can't talk to you right now. You're grounded.'

Mum had picked a great time to demonstrate awareness of American film-type stuff. No Porsche convertibles, no allowance, no malls, no driving-at-sixteen, no living-near-a-beach – but grounded?

I sat in my room all Saturday, unable to believe it. It was so unfair. It was Fireworks Night! The one night of the year there would have been ... fireworks! And getting-into-a-warm-bath-type hugging! Apparently I wasn't even allowed out to the leisure centre display tomorrow night either, the one my family was going to.

I had to text Luke to say I couldn't come out with the Taylors. I wasn't strong enough to speak to him yet, having left things so strangely at his house.

At dinner, Mum slammed my portion of pasta down onto my plate. Jamie paused mid-mouthful and looked, wonderingly, from me to Mum. We'd never gone in for open tension before.

'What—' he began.

'Shut up,' I said at once.

Ivy flashed me a worried look.

She came upstairs after the meal and stuck her head round the door.

'Hey, what's wrong?'

'Mum found out about Luke.'

'Oh my God,' said Ivy with evident horror. 'That's so scary.'

I nodded mutely.

'Oh, thanks for sorting out my essay,' Ivy said. 'Don't say anything, will you?'

'Of course not.'

'Maybe I'll repay the favour one day.'

'Next time I need you to impersonate me in a netball game, I'll get you to come back from uni.'

She came over and put her hand on my shoulder in support, then left. I couldn't believe I had thought for ages that I would be watching the fireworks in the dark with Luke right now, and actually I was alone in my bedroom. He hadn't texted me back, although

I was trying to pretend I hadn't noticed. And I was barely speaking to Poppy, although I really wanted to sort things out with her. We'd been on the verge of a reconciliation at her house, until I'd realised Luke and Claudia were in the kitchen together. Claudia was permanently there these days, I had learned that much. In fact there was only one time I could think of when I'd be able to talk to Poppy alone.

About ten minutes later I knocked timidly on Ivy's door. She opened it and laughed as I stepped inside in my winter coat, scarf and gloves.

'Do you want me to ask Mum?'

'What?'

'About putting the heating on.'

'No,' I said. 'It's not that. I was hoping you could repay that favour.'

OK, climbing out of Ivy's window was a bit dramatic, but it was the only way I could think of to sort things. I had carefully done a teen-film-type assessment of sneaking out through my own room, unaided, but my conclusion had been less than promising:

Checklist for Sneaking Out in Manner of American Teen-Film:

- *Cover your tracks with a handy piece of kit, e.g. life-sized doll in bed, recorded snoring noises etc.*
- *Use new-looking, gently sloping roof outside your window to easily climb down some trellis into a conveniently placed, non-spiky bush.*

Comment:

- *Do not own life-sized doll. Or recording equipment. Only sound-generating activity in my room is the rowing machine. Hearing sounds of rowing machine activity would bring family running in amazement.*
- *Only option is inconvenient and dirty scramble out of skylight and across South London roof, followed by vertiginous drop to front garden.*

However, I did have one thing. A sister who owed me a favour, and whose bedroom window was above the porch.

As the bus headed towards the park where the fireworks were happening, I rubbed my bruises from the climb. Even though they were on top of the bruises from trying to jump over the vaulting horse in PE, I felt sort of soothed already. It was a bit stupid to risk even more trouble by sneaking out, but could things with Mum really get any worse? My ticket had sat tantalizingly on my desk. And Claudia was at the fireworks in Kensington with her dad. No, this was the perfect window of opportunity to speak to Poppy.

There were crowds of people because the fireworks were about to start, but eventually I spotted Poppy, wearing the bright red beret I had given her for Christmas last year. Her mum was handing out jacket potatoes in the background while talking to a familiar-looking, tall boy with blond hair. Jez! The boy Poppy had a huge crush on earlier this year, who had gone out with Claudia! Of course, it was a youth club event, and that's where Poppy knew him from.

Poppy caught sight of me. 'I didn't think you were coming,' she said, coldly. 'Luke said about your mum. I suppose you've sneaked out?'

'Yes, she doesn't know I'm here,' I explained, looking around for Luke. He must have gone for drinks with Mr Taylor or something.

I thought for a minute it was all going to be OK, but Poppy said annoyingly, 'Where did you disappear to last night?'

Oh yes.

'Sorry. I was really upset. I had this argument with Luke, and—'

Poppy rolled her eyes. 'It's all about Luke these days, isn't it? I expect you're here to see him now?'

'No, I came here to see you!'

'Well, here I am,' said Poppy. 'We can talk while he's on the Big Wheel with Claudia.'

What?

I felt like I'd been punched.

'But Claudia's with her dad this weekend,' I said helplessly, as if saying this adamantly enough might make it true.

'Claudia was at my house when she found out this morning that her dad has to work this weekend. My mum had a spare ticket, so she offered it to Claudia.'

Oh God. I would have to politely explain to Poppy's mum that she needed to stop being nice to Claudia.

I looked over at the Big Wheel, silhouetted against the fireworks starting to go off. My stomach plummeted with dread. As I started to run towards the Big Wheel, Poppy cried after me, 'So, you came to see me then?'

I stopped and turned. 'What?'

'I nearly believed you for a minute!'

What, was I supposed to ignore the fact that Claudia and Luke were alone together on the Big Wheel?

Poppy laughed, 'What I like is how innocent you act. You say you're here to make up with me, but you're not. It just proves your priorities.'

I'd had enough. 'Do you really need that much attention?' I said, my voice going high with the effort of not bursting into tears. 'Is that why you're spending time with Claudia again – to put you in the centre of a struggle, so you can feel important?'

'Claudia is there for me,' said Poppy, with a dangerous air of calm. 'To you, a boyfriend is clearly more important than a friendship.'

I gulped and started running again towards the Big Wheel, managing only to look back and say, 'I didn't realise I had to make a choice.'

As I approached the wheel I caught sight of Luke. The Big Wheel had stopped momentarily, and he was right up at the top. The night sky was lit up with red and golden sparkles, the shimmer reflected in the metal frame of the Big Wheel. For a minute I could barely distinguish Claudia because she was sat so close to him, her dark hair almost merging into the fabric of his jacket and the night sky. It was windy, but of course they weren't cold, because they were together. I was the one out in the cold. Claudia had stolen my fantasy: to be wrapped up warm by Luke on Fireworks Night.

Breathing hard, I turned and walked away, until I was alone in the quiet darkness of the park, only the distant hum of fairground generators in the background. I couldn't believe this was actually happening to me. I needed to speak to Luke and find out what was going on. Then everything would be OK.

I dialled Luke's number, praying he would answer. If it went through to voicemail, I would be sick.

Fortunately he picked up quickly, sounding surprised. 'Holly!'

'Luke, it's me,' I said superfluously. I was so relieved he had answered. I cleared my throat to bring my voice under control, because it sounded shaky. Something made me want to act normal. After all Luke didn't even know I was out. None of this was real yet, not really. Not until I made it real.

'What are you up to?' said Luke.

'Nothing much. What about you?'

'I'm on the Big Wheel,' said Luke. 'There's a great view.'

I felt a rush of relief and warmth. I was such an idiot, worrying about him.

'You're not up there with another girl, are you?' I was relieved enough to tease him. Of course I could trust him. He was so honest. I had been overly paranoid and—

'No, don't worry,' said Luke, 'I'm all by myself.'

First Cut is the Deepest

Ways That This Could Still Be OK and Luke Hadn't Actually Lied to Me

1. I got the wrong number and called somebody else, also called Luke, and also on a Big Wheel.
2. In between me seeing Luke and Claudia, and him saying he was alone, Claudia had sadly fallen from the Big Wheel and was now hanging suspended in mid-air by her hair, which had become badly tangled around one of the Big Wheel spokes (causing an irreversible bald spot).
3. Luke had not noticed Claudia was even with him because she was so indistinguished.

But who was I trying to kid? It was awful. Just awful.

There was a rustling noise and I heard Claudia giggle in the background, then Luke went, 'Holly–'

But I was already hanging up, frozen.

I don't know how I got onto a bus. I didn't even realise I was crying until one of the old ladies who had helped me with my maths gave me a tissue, which just made me cry more.

She said, 'Mascara's never a good idea when you've been crying, is it?'

I looked blearily at my reflection in the bus window and had to agree with her.

Which was when something clicked.

Yesterday, when Claudia had been crying on Luke, she should have had make-up running down her face, looking terrible! She always, always wore tons of make-up. Eyeliner, mascara and eye-shadow.

But there had been nothing.

Oh my God. When Claudia had gone to the bathroom at Poppy's, she had taken off her make-up! That's why she had looked so washed-out when she got back into the living room, the first time! She had done it on purpose in order not to look terrible when she cried all over Luke! She knew he was about to come home, because I had told her. She had planned her reaction to the so-called phone call, the tears, the whole thing!

'Are you OK?' said the old lady, looking alarmed at my shocked face.

But I stood to get off the bus, wide-eyed with disbelief.

Then, when I was walking down Rosehill Road, Luke phoned! I picked up without saying anything. It sounded like he was walking somewhere quiet.

'Holly, what's going on? Poppy says you're here at the fireworks?'

I did a cross between a snort and a sob. 'Yes, I was, but you were busy.'

'Look, Holly—'

'There's not very much you can say,' I interrupted. I stopped in the dark, still street, and rubbed my head because it was aching. I wished someone was there to hug me.

'I know you lied to me about it, because I was there,' I managed to continue, my voice muted by incredulity that we were actually having this conversation. 'I saw you on the Big Wheel, with your arms round Claudia.'

I mean, had he kissed her on the Big Wheel, just before I saw them? Or before I had even suspected anything?

'But—'

'No. You clearly don't want to be with me any more. I trusted you. But now it's ruined.'

I looked down at my phone, his name still illuminated on the little screen, and with that I hung up on him. On Luke. The boy who used to be my boyfriend, for whom I'd gone through all that confrontation with my mum. All for nothing.

Back home after a sleepless night, I was still trying to clear my head. But the truth was, I preferred it jumbled, because no one warned you about the sheer, plummeting misery of breaking up with someone. God, this was new. It was like a physical pain. Were people seriously expected to go to school and carry on as if there was space in their heads for Shakespeare and equations? It was precisely the opposite of the sinking-into-a-warm-bath feeling. Now the water had gone cold and the bubbles had popped. All that time I had been torturing myself about Luke and Claudia, yet I hadn't really believed there had been anything going on. Not until now. I just thought she was after him. But I had thought I could trust Luke, and I had been totally wrong. God, Claudia had even heard him lie to me! I bet she was still laughing now!

In the end I called Sasha, who said she was going to come round, which was really sweet of her, given that she lived miles away.

After all, I couldn't call Poppy to talk about it, because it was suddenly, dismally clear that she'd known all about it all, and approved. After all, Poppy had known Claudia was up on the Big Wheel with Luke! Poppy had tried to call me, once, but I hadn't answered and she hadn't left a voicemail. Clearly she had never thought I was good enough for Luke. I had been making an idiot of myself, trying to make up with her.

I had thought Luke was so honest, so totally trustworthy, yet he had deliberately deceived me. And there was nothing he could say to deny it.

Good Things About Life

- *I'm alive and I have both my legs and stuff.*
- *I have my own bedroom.*

Bad Things About Life (Worst Three Only, to Save Paper)

- *I am really ugly from crying, with purple bags under my eyes.*
- *Luke hasn't called me since I hung up on him.*

- *I've got absolutely nothing to do for the next forty years, so I might as well not exist.*

I'd just put down the pen when Sasha walked in the door! That was quick.

'Did my mum let you in?' I said in surprise.

'No, Ivy did. Your mum must be out.'

Oh yes, she would be swimming at the leisure centre.

I turned the radio off. 'Can't they have non-love songs for sad people?' I said. 'They're all about love.'

'What else is there to sing about?' said Sasha.

'I don't know.'

'Maybe chocolate or something,' Sasha said thoughtfully as she took off a huge coat and about three scarves and sat on the end of the bed. Having assessed the temperature of the room, she put two of the scarves straight back on.

'What, like, "All You Need is Chocolate"? Or "Chocolate Lifts You Up Where You Belong"?'

'Exactly.'

Sasha peered over the edge of my bed at my school books, and then at my list.

'Also, your homework has gone all wrinkly from where you've cried on it,' she added helpfully.

I obediently added this to the Bad Things column. We sat and stared at my list together in silence.

'Kind of puts the ice cream argument into perspective, I guess,' said Sasha.

'How did you get here so fast?'

'Darren dropped me off.'

124

'I didn't know he had a licence already.'

'Oh, he doesn't,' said Sasha casually, 'but his older brother was out and Darren knows where he keeps the keys. Oh, his friends have offered to trash Claudia's house, if you like.'

'That's so sweet,' I said and blinked back tears.

'Is your mum still angry with you?'

I thought about it, miserably. 'She's barely talking to me.'

'Does she know . . .'

'No,' I said. 'She doesn't know I've seen Luke since I was grounded. She doesn't even know I went out to the fireworks.'

It was ironic, because when I had got back in, I had just let myself in the front door, really not caring any more who saw me. I don't know why, but in a weird way I had even wanted Mum to come out into the hall and see that I was crying and ask what was wrong. But Mum had been at Mrs Heathfield's and Dad had been in the bathroom and I had been able to get all the way upstairs to my loft room without even a light going on.

'Has Luke phoned you?'

I shook my head. I had turned my phone on again that morning, hoping for a barrage of texts and missed calls from him that a) explained that I'd just got it all wrong, like that time on the bus when Luke didn't see me, and b) said how sorry he was and how actually I was the most important person to him in the universe, but – nothing.

'I hate Claudia so much,' I said. 'She's ruined my life. It's all her fault. All of it.'

Sasha nodded and said, 'Yes. Well – no, but I know what you mean.'

That was a bit disloyal. I gave her a quizzical look. I was quite happy to blame Claudia for everything.

'Well, OK,' said Sasha, 'the fact that Claudia's on the Big Wheel with your boyfriend, and pretends to be upset around him and all that – that's her fault. But you can't really blame her for the stuff with your mum and with Poppy!'

I tried unsuccessfully not to sulk. It wasn't my fault if my family compelled me to lie, was it? Or if Claudia stole Poppy away! I went quiet and ate a Hula Hoop.

'You need to eat proper, balanced meals,' Sasha said in concern, eyeing my Hula Hoops and the Double Decker bar nearby.

'This is a balanced meal,' I said defensively. 'Something sweet, something savoury.'

'I think I'll go,' said Sasha, sounding irritated. 'Listen, I only said that about Claudia so you can sort it out. Not everything is somebody else's fault, you know.'

'How will you get home?'

'I'll get the bus.'

With that she stropped out, standing on my biology homework as she left! How dare Sasha be so horrible to me when I was upset, instead of supporting me? What was I supposed to do now?

I picked up my biology homework (already wrinkled from being cried on, and now trodden on, too). It was the stupid stuff about pheromones. As I read it, something became depressingly clear. Nature made sure you stayed close to the people with whom you had essential relationships. Yet there were no pheromones for friends! I had thought friendships were essential, but clearly they could be dissolved in the blink of an eye. Maybe Claudia had actually got it right, about not giving friends too much priority.

Maybe I had to resign myself to my family. It was the only permanent bond, wasn't it? I remembered how delighted I had made Mum when she thought I wanted to play football. She had been proud, and hugged me, and for a moment I had belonged.

That was when Mum knocked on the door and stepped inside, her hair still slightly wet from her swim.

Surprised, I looked up.

'I'm going for a short run in a minute. Do you want to come?'

'Why are you talking to me?' I said suspiciously. All I'd had for the last few days were the basics. You know, was it you who moved the scissors? Why on earth can't you tidy your trainers away in the same place every time? Do you realise that that melted chocolate took ages to get out of your school shoe? And so on.

'I heard from Ivy that you helped her with her essay,' said Mum.

'Oh,' I said, because I didn't know what else to say.

Mum didn't say well done or anything, but her expression had softened slightly. She said, 'Anyway, don't worry about the run.'

'No, hang on.' I thought about it. 'Definitely just a short run?'

She nodded impatiently and was already halfway out the door again when I called out, 'Yes. OK.'

Light My Fire

OK, I didn't enjoy the run. Probably because I have always hated jogging. And by the time we passed Poppy's house, Mum was already ahead of me by a few paces. But it felt like a necessary penance. I had to try and fit in with my family. Otherwise, where was I going to belong? Although I was already a 100% social failure, I still had quite a bit of my life left to go. I thought back to when Mum had confirmed I was definitely part of the family and realised something. Absurdly, behind the relief had been disappointment. It would have explained why I was different, when actually, there was no one to blame but myself.

Suddenly I realised with dread that we were running to Kestrel Hill. I was OK until we started running up to the little hut, which vividly brought back the memory of Luke and me watching the light pollution. Suddenly I stumbled on the rough path and, even though it was only a scratch, I started crying.

The thing is, I wasn't just crying about that. Everything was coming out – Luke, Poppy, Sasha, everything. Mum sighed and looked exasperated. She didn't even know that she had got what she wanted: Luke and I had split up.

'What is it?' Mum said as I cried some more.

I couldn't think of anything to pretend to be crying about. And my knee hurt. So I said, 'I'm not friends with Poppy any more. Or Sasha. And I went out last night and Luke was with someone else. So we've broken up.'

Trouble was, I could barely tell the story, I was crying so much. By the time I had finished, my knee had stopped bleeding so I stood up again, snuffling to myself. 'So. You've got what you wanted.'

Mum sighed and said, not unkindly, 'You think I wanted this?'

I shrugged.

'Look, this is exactly the kind of thing I was worried about.'

I must have looked puzzled because she continued, 'I mean, when I said you were too young. It's hard when it doesn't last. You know, I had my first relationship when I was about your age.'

I stopped sobbing in shock. 'What did you say?'

She stated this completely factually, as if she was talking about a badminton score or something.

'Well, I was a bit older: eighteen. I was so upset when it ended! I nearly failed my exams – it could even have affected me getting into uni. You go into these things and don't realise how awful you'll feel when it doesn't work out. And the younger you are when it happens, the more of a shock it is.'

I guess she had a very small point. Without necessarily thinking Luke and I would last forever, neither had I considered that we might break up, or how devastated I would feel.

'Of course, you can't not have a relationship because you're scared of the bit at the end,' Mum added. 'But anyway – that's why

I was worried. Your dad and I don't want you to get hurt. Or to . . .
to compromise your future. Relationships with boys can get . . .
serious, you know. Quite quickly. Lots of teenage girls end up as
single mothers, you know, it happens a lot.'

She is so embarrassing.

'But you just got angry,' I said.

Mum was quiet for a bit and then she said, 'I was surprised. You
lied to me. I need to know where you are, for safety if nothing else.
If you say you're at football and you're not—'

I swallowed my irritation and said with some relief, 'That
wasn't me, that was Poppy.'

Mum frowned. 'You chose to carry on lying, Holly, instead of
having a difficult conversation. That's all there is to it!'

'It wasn't like that. I didn't want you to get all angry and –
upset, and stuff, when it wasn't even a big deal.'

'But because you'd lied, you made it worse. I felt I couldn't trust
you at all!'

I wanted to scream, because I had half thought we were going
to have a normal conversation, and now she was being all strict
and annoying again. But then her words triggered something
small in my head. It was true that being lied to was not much fun.

She continued, 'I mean, it made me wonder if you had been
lying about other stuff.'

'I wasn't lying about other stuff!' I said, surprised.

'Well, I can see that now, because I've had time to calm down.'

'I know I should have told you,' I said miserably. 'I was scared.
And I told myself I was just, you know, withholding small bits of
information. And that way, I wasn't really deceiving you, and no
one was getting hurt.'

Mum snorted.

'I know, I was lying. And it's my fault Poppy lied about the football, too. I was just scared of the confrontation.'

'You're just like your dad. He prefers not to confront things.'

'So we are definitely related, then?' I laughed weakly.

Mum looked shocked. 'You're not still thinking about that mad idea?'

'No,' I said. It was clear he was my dad. 'Just checking.'

Then, Mum suddenly gave me a hug!

Afterwards, she said, 'You're definitely a Stockwell. And I don't think you're the only one who tells the occasional lie. I always knew when your brother pretended he was washing his hands before dinner, but actually he was just running the tap.'

'Er, I think he still does that.'

'And I remember when you were little and we heard ice cream van music, I always used to tell you the music meant—'

'That they'd run out of ice cream,' I finished. 'I remember that.'

'But let's be honest on the major points,' said Mum. 'OK? That way we'll be OK in the long run.'

'What long run?' I said, panicked. Then I realised what she'd said and said, 'Oh. Yes.'

'Let's go home,' said Mum. 'It's getting a bit cold. We'll put the heating on.'

November Rain

So, things were OK with Mum again. However, how was I going to get through school without any friends? The downside of it being Christmassy and cold was that if you were depressed, it made everything even worse.

I prayed to somehow get Monday off school, but nothing happened. I had to get the early bus in the dark for Extra English, and the driver didn't stop at the bus stop, despite me ringing on the bell! So I had to walk through the rain, in the dark, with no umbrella and just my scarf pulled up over my head. Basically, I felt like my life was going to end.

To top it all off, we had PE.

'Right girls, let's go,' said Mrs Mastiff, when everyone was assembled.

'But it's raining,' I said quickly. 'Mrs Craignish said—'

'Mrs Craignish isn't here,' said Mrs Mastiff with a note of triumph, keeping an eye on the staffroom window. 'She's got a cold. OK girls, move quickly!'

'What about Health and Safety?' I said hopefully.

I can't really repeat what Mrs Mastiff said.

So we all went out to the netball court in the rain. I noticed Poppy was zigzagging to avoid the raindrops again. It reminded me of how things had been before all this trouble with Luke. Had he really been worth it?

As everyone shivered around the court, Mrs Mastiff shouted things like, 'Come on, girls!' and, 'What doesn't kill you makes you stronger!'

Only the really die-hard sporty people actually appeared to be enjoying it. I was so purple with cold that I risked blending in to my purple and grey PE kit.

Mrs Mastiff said sarcastically, 'Holly, it doesn't count as netball if you stand still throughout the game and swivel half-heartedly on one foot when I look at you.'

The worst thing was that I couldn't just have a laugh with Poppy or Sasha because neither of them were talking to me. I'd been blanking them right back. I couldn't decide whether I was more numb with cold or with misery.

Only English to go, and then I could go home and hide under my duvet. We had all scrambled to sit as near to the radiators as possible after PE, and Mrs Mitford was making us read bits from *Julius Caesar*.

Jo went first and read for a bit, concluding, *'Et tu Brute?/Then fall Caesar.'*

'Good,' said Mrs Mitford. 'As I said, this phrase represents the

133

betrayal felt by Caesar. Brutus was his friend and ally, yet at the end is betrayed by him. Holly, would you read the next section?'

I knew she would pick me. She was pretty soft, but, she had still noticed that I had missed that Extra English lesson to see Luke.

As I stood up, I realised with sheer horror that my eyes were filling with tears. (Either that or Mrs Mitford had just gone all blurry?) The subject of betrayal was just too close to home.

'Are you OK?' said Mrs Mitford.

Her being nice was the final straw.

It was awful. Even more awful than all the other awful things that had happened. I tried to blink furiously, but it was no good. And my tears were more about how betrayed I felt by Poppy and Sasha, than for Luke.

'Poppy,' said Mrs Mitford quietly, 'can you take Holly to get a glass of water?'

Oh no. They should have some way of letting teachers know crucial information about who was no longer friends with whom. A notice board in the staffroom entitled: *No Longer Has Any Friends*, perhaps. With my name on it.

I opened my mouth to claim I was OK, but Poppy stood and said, 'Yes, Mrs Mitford.'

I followed her out of the room and tried to stop crying.

Poppy shut the classroom door, got a glass of water from the drinking fountain and handed it to me. 'Where's a hot chocolate machine when you need one?'

I smiled, although the smile felt diluted, like weak orange squash. She was clearly working at being nice.

'I don't know how it all went so wrong,' I managed, looking

134

around at the silent corridor. It was a bit surreal being out of lessons.

'I saw you jogging with your mum yesterday,' said Poppy. 'I was, like, has it come to this?'

I snorted through my tears.

Poppy paused, then she said something amazing. 'Look, I didn't know Claudia was after Luke. I had no idea.'

What?

'But – at the fireworks – I thought you knew.'

Poppy looked horrified. 'No! I knew they were on the Big Wheel together. But that's all.'

'Oh my God.' My shock and curiosity overcame my crying. 'Why didn't you say something yesterday?'

'I phoned you and you didn't answer! Then I saw Sasha walking down the road so I figured you just wanted to talk to her. Then I was going to say something this morning and you totally blanked me!'

'What happened?'

'Claudia asked Luke if he would go on the Big Wheel, to help get some distance between her and Jez. You know, what with Jez being her ex. So then you turned up and ran off and the next thing I knew, Luke was back, with Claudia behind him trying to keep up, and he was, like, 'Was Holly here?' So I said yes, of course, and asked him what had happened, and he just strode off towards the exit! Then Claudia told me about Luke claiming he was alone. She was smirking about it, so I got angry with her and my mum ended up calling her a cab. I don't think she'll be so keen to take her under her wing again.'

Blimey. There I was, thinking Claudia had probably slept

over at Poppy's and they'd all stayed up late watching films and stuff!

'I'm furious with Claudia,' Poppy continued. 'I should never have started speaking to her again. But it was like she was there again at the right time, when I was angry with you about the bowling.'

'She knew we weren't getting on,' I said, 'Mrs Mastiff was going on about it in PE that time, remember?'

And, now I came to think of it, she had waited until I was upset about Luke to win me over, too.

I told Poppy about how Claudia taken her make-up off so she could cry on Luke without her make-up running!

'Oh my God,' said Poppy.

'And then my mum found out about Luke.'

'Oh my God!'

'I wanted to say sorry for having disappeared on Friday night. That was why I sneaked out to the fireworks! But I was so worried about Luke being with Claudia.'

'Well I can see that now,' said Poppy. 'I was angry because I just felt like our friendship didn't mean much to you. I thought Claudia was right, that you had only been friends with me to get Luke.'

'When did she say that?' I said, outraged.

'At her house. When you went to the loo.'

See? See? I was never going to the loo at someone's house again, ever.

'You didn't seriously think—'

'It was the way she put it. You know, you'd been seeing so much of Luke that, if she were me, she would draw her own conclusions.'

God. I felt awful.

'I'm sorry that I prioritised him, a bit. It was stupid. But I've been friends with you for ages! It wasn't ever because of Luke!'

'There's something else,' said Poppy. 'Look, I don't want to make a big deal out of it when you're upset, but when you said I was jealous, I got really annoyed.'

'But you said that! Claudia told me!'

'What, that I was feeling jealous? I never told her that!'

We looked at each other, slightly shocked.

'But, she told me,' I said. 'In confidence. You felt neglected and jealous because I was spending so much time with Luke.'

'No! Well, OK, a bit. But I didn't talk to her about it. I didn't say anything to anyone! Look, Holly, you've fancied Luke for ages. I was really happy for you. It was just hard when I was used to us spending lots of time together. I did try to act like I was OK, but I wasn't.'

'I was really annoyed that you were talking to Claudia about me, behind my back,' I said.

'That's what I thought you were doing about me!' Poppy exclaimed.

Wow. Claudia had methodically taken advantage of the arguments Poppy and I had been having. She was totally trying to make us both insecure!

'And all that stuff about your family!' added Poppy. 'What was that?'

'To make me even more paranoid?' I said, thinking, well, it worked.

I looked at the closed classroom door. Only Mrs Mitford would allow us this much time out of a lesson. It was just as well, because I had something difficult to say. I took a deep breath. 'OK, so

Claudia's been taking advantage of the situation. But it wasn't just her, was it? I sabotaged things too. I'm sorry about, you know, making you lie. I've sorted all that out with Mum now.'

'It's just that you seemed so worried about it, initially,' said Poppy, 'and you said you were just working up to telling your mum the truth. But then you seemed to get used to lying and I just thought, Oh God, is this going to go on forever? And you were convincing yourself it wasn't that bad.'

'But it was.'

'Exactly.'

I thought back. 'I didn't realise it was the lying that was annoying you. I thought you were jealous.'

'Also,' said Poppy, sounding really worked up again, 'I had to be so careful! I couldn't call your house, or even go to the shop, because your mum might have seen me and it would have got you into trouble. I felt like a prisoner in my bedroom!'

'I feel terrible,' I said. 'I'm so sorry – I didn't realise you felt like that.' I gulped a bit. 'I've been rubbish. I thought things were so black and white, blaming Claudia for everything. But actually they are a bit . . .'

'Greyer?'

'Yes.'

'More textured,' I said in Mrs Leyton's voice, and we laughed, quietly in case Mrs Mitford heard.

'Claudia hates you,' said Poppy. 'Well, resents is probably a better word. It's like you've got all this stuff she wanted.'

'But she didn't do all this just to get Luke?'

'No,' said Poppy. 'I reckon she does really want proper friends. She just has no idea how to treat them. Luke was just there, wasn't he? Another challenge. She can't relate to boys on any other level.'

Poppy is the opposite, typically she can only relate to boys as friends. Which is why she never managed to get together with Jez, who I always thought was perfect for her. But I didn't say anything.

'Er – you know, I don't think Claudia and Luke are together?' said Poppy suddenly.

It was funny. I always thought 'chocolate' and 'weekend' were the best words in the English language, but suddenly they had competition.

'What do you mean, you don't think they're together?'

'Well, Luke didn't pay her the slightest bit of attention when he was trying to call you at Fireworks Night. And I haven't heard them speaking on the phone or anything. Then again, I'm not talking to Claudia any more, so I can't find out.'

Oh yes, the downside of not talking to somebody.

'Could we ask Bethan?' I said, inspired.

'Yes,' said Poppy, 'but then she'd tell everybody that we'd asked her, and . . .'

'OK, good point. Well, could you ask Luke?'

'Why don't you ask Luke?' said Poppy, as if this was very amusing.

'No way! If he doesn't want to talk to me, then . . .'

'I reckon he does, though. He came up to the bus stop today and then looked disappointed.'

'So?'

'So he was disappointed because you had Extra English and weren't there!'

'Poppy, he could have been disappointed for any number of reasons! Like, he could have just missed a bus, or he'd forgotten his packed lunch or something.'

We fell silent. Then Poppy grinned at me and gave me a hug. I hugged her back.

The bell rang and everyone streamed out. Mrs Mitford appeared at the door.

'Do you feel better, Holly?'

I wasn't sure. Did I?

Don't Look Back in Anger

I sat in my room pretending to do my art homework. It was brilliant, things being OK with Poppy again. However, I was a bundle of nerves trying to decide how I felt about Luke and Claudia not being together. It wasn't just because of Claudia that we had split up, was it? More than anything, I felt betrayed. He had intentionally deceived me.

OK. If he came to me, I would talk to him, but boys were not the be all and end all of life.

With that decided, I actually got some of my self-portrait done, boldly putting in a bit more cross-hatching and texture. Halfway through, Ivy came in.

'I got a good mark!' she announced. 'In my essay, I mean.'

'That's brilliant!'

'Thanks again for your help. Er – I hear you've sorted things out with Mum,' Ivy continued. 'Was it a nightmare?'

'Ish. Well, no, not terrible, actually.'

'I just can't imagine it,' said Ivy.

'Well, you're lucky you don't have anything to conceal.'

Ivy looked at me for a minute, then went back and shut the door, before perching on the exercise bike. She sighed heavily. 'OK – look, we both know what she's like, right? So I just pretend, you know, like it doesn't exist. And we both stay happy. I never even told her about me and Amit . . .'

My jaw dropped. Amit had done fencing with Ivy at the leisure centre before she went to uni! I remembered seeing the team photos.

'We went out for ten weeks,' said Ivy, half laughing at my face.

Oh my God, I couldn't believe she'd had a long-term relationship and I hadn't known about it!

'I just never said anything,' said Ivy. 'It was easy. We just saw each other after fencing. Or even,' she paused to giggle, '*instead* of fencing.'

'No!' I said, shocked. I knew how obsessively sporty Ivy was. I couldn't believe she had given up sport to see a boy, or that she had been calmly keeping all this stuff from us!

Ivy giggled, presumably at my disbelief, or maybe from releasing the tension of keeping quiet.

'Why didn't you tell me?' I said, a bit hurt. I could have kept it a secret!

'I didn't want to put you under pressure to lie about it. Anyway, I'm going out with Jack now. Bloke from uni. That's why I decided to come home to do my essay, so I could focus on it. Otherwise I'd be straight round to his flat!'

'Right,' I said slowly. I couldn't believe it!

After Ivy had left, I added a bit more texture to my self-portrait (some inadvertent, due to unexpected sneezing). I bet I had got this cold from PE in the rain.

After my third sneeze, I suddenly heard a murmur from downstairs. The murmur of two people talking. It was Luke. Luke! Talking to my mum! Oh my God. I raced down two flights of stairs, jumped the last few steps and went straight into panic mode.

'We'll go for a walk,' I said as I looked wildly for my trainers. Why on earth couldn't I tidy them away in the same place every time?

'It's cold,' said Mum. 'You can sit in the front room for five minutes.'

What?

I almost looked outside for the hidden TV crew, but contented myself with eyeing Mum uneasily as Luke followed me into the front room and shut the door.

'Poppy said she'd talked to you,' said Luke, in an urgent tone.

'What, about you not going out with Claudia?'

'Yes!'

'Does that change anything?'

His face fell.

'Why didn't you come round sooner?' I said.

'I didn't want to get you into any more trouble with your mum,' said Luke, looking taken aback. 'But I wanted to talk to you face to face. So I was hoping I'd bump into you on the bus this morning. I waited around and stuff but—'

'I had Extra English,' I said.

'Yes, Poppy said that, just now. And she told me that you'd talked to your mum about me! So I came over.'

'So what happened?' I said sharply. 'I saw you and Claudia, you know. Sitting really close on the Big Wheel.'

'I know. It wasn't supposed to be like that. When the ride started moving Claudia was just joking around, you know, about me needing a cord for my gloves?'

What? That conversation was between me and Luke! It wasn't something she was supposed to calmly steal!

'Claudia, like, leaned over and put her hands in both my pockets and said teasingly that she was checking I hadn't lost my gloves,' Luke continued. 'Actually, she squished my jacket potato. But I wasn't going to climb off the Big Wheel from high up in the air, was I? And then when you called, Claudia was unbelievable! When I said I was alone, she deliberately made a noise. She was clearly trying to sabotage things!'

'I did hear something,' I said, thinking back.

'And then she tried to snog me,' said Luke.

'What?' I said, horrified.

'Oh, I thought you saw,' said Luke sheepishly. 'But it didn't happen.'

Ouch. Ouch. Ouch.

'Sorry, I wanted to tell you the truth.'

I took a deep breath. 'But you lied to me,' I said, the hurt rising back to the surface. Luke looked all forlorn. But did he think I was an idiot? 'Why did you say you were alone? I need to be able to trust you.'

'I'm sorry,' Luke said simply. He sat down on Mum's recently restrung badminton racquet and hastily stood up again. 'It was so stupid. I didn't think it through, there wasn't any time. I didn't plan it like that.'

'You should have just said. You know, told me the truth.'

Luke sounded despairing. 'Holly, you really hate her. You were saying about not being able to go to the loo in case she talked about you—'

'Listen, I should never have mentioned that—'

144

'No, but, you were grounded as well! I thought you were stuck at home and we were out. I knew it would make you feel worse! I was trying to avoid another argument. You got so upset before – you know, with the work experience and everything. I thought if I didn't say Claudia was there, no one would get hurt. But I just made it seem worse than it was. Nothing's going on.'

He looked at me. Something small twigged inside my head. Was this how Mum had felt? Her picturing me on my way to single motherhood, when actually Luke and I had been standing in a garden shed with somebody turning a light bulb on and off?

Luke stood up. 'Look, I'll go. But I'm telling you the truth now, OK? I was just scared of how you would react.'

That's what I had done too, lied just because I was scared.

He had half opened the door when I said, carefully, 'I don't like it when you're not a happy penguin.'

'What?'

I walked over and shut the door again.

'I'm not going to kiss you because I've got a cold,' I said. 'But I will, soon.'

As he came over and gave me a big hug, I realised I was going to be a bit more balanced about him in future. But it felt brilliant to be together again! He had been stupid, but I had been stupid too.

After Luke had gone, I steeled myself then went into the kitchen to face Mum. She put the kettle on and got out the hot chocolate, all without speaking. I tried to assess whether it was a good silence or a bad silence.

145

'I can just go to Luke's house in future, if you prefer?' I said tentatively.

'No,' Mum said. 'He can come here again if you like.'

Miracles never cease!

'But he's not allowed in your room,' she said clearly. 'And I'd prefer you didn't shut the living room door.'

God, how embarrassing.

'We've made up, anyway,' I said, allowing myself a big smile. I couldn't suppress it any longer.

'You look happier,' said Mum, looking faintly won round.

'Did you know,' I added hopefully, playing my *pièce de résistance*, 'when Luke was a baby, his first word was "ball".'

Mum seemed to approve of this.

'What was my first word?' I asked.

She thought about it as she made my drink and then said, 'Cake.'

With a Little Help
From My Friends

Five weeks later Ivy came home for Christmas and Dad and I helped her carry her bags up to her room.

'How's Extra English going?' said Ivy.

'Quite well.'

'Mum said you were getting really good marks?'

'I was a bit behind for a bit, but it's back on track now.'

Ivy was wearing a tinsel garland, for some reason. She took it off and draped it ceremoniously around my neck. I giggled.

Once Dad and I had dumped Ivy's bags on the floor of her little boxroom, he went downstairs to lock up the car. I shut Ivy's bedroom door.

'You should tell Mum about Jack,' I said.

Ivy sat down on the bed and shook her head with surprising vehemence. 'No,' she said, 'I can't! Not now.'

'But you know, Mum said she was just worried about us getting hurt.'

Ivy seemed to be considering it, but then said, 'No – I've just never said anything! It's stupid, really. I know she's not been too bad about you, in the end. So I could just say. But – I don't know – I've spent ages concealing all this from her. It's too late to go back.'

'It's such a big part of your life to keep quiet.'

Ivy sighed. 'I'm used to it now.'

'And you're going to keep it up indefinitely,' I said as I headed for the door. It wasn't really a question, more of a statement. Ivy nodded.

Upstairs I looked in my mirror and arranged my tinsel garland around my head. It looked cool, in a Nativity-play-angel-type way. I couldn't believe that all this time I thought Mum and Ivy were as close as anything, and actually there was this barrier between them. An invisible one. And for a change, being sporty had nothing to do with whether you could vault over it or not.

Despite the imminent Christmas holidays, we still had school! Fortunately Mrs Mitford was so worried that I might cry again that she never asked me anything any more. Therefore I was safe to use English lessons to organise my Christmas shopping list:

Examples of the Struggle Between Fate and Free Will in Julius Caesar

Mum: vouchers for Foot Locker
Dad: golf calendar

Ivy:	*Bend it Like Beckham DVD (which she said she hadn't seen either. What was the world coming to?)*
Jamie:	*football-shaped chocolates*
Grandma:	*Body Shop soaps*
Poppy:	*hairclip from TopShop*
Sasha:	*bright pink scarf from TopShop*
Luke:	*???*

Hmm. Boys were really complicated to buy for. (Except for Jamie. We had a long-established understanding that we didn't know what the other wanted and always got each other chocolate.)

Also, Year Ten still had to do netball. Clearly, life could be going brilliantly well in nearly all respects, but there was no escaping PE. We all got changed and waited outside in the crisp winter sunshine for Mrs Mastiff to show up. Claudia was on the edge of the group, moaning to Bethan about her mum having returned from filming! After having acted so needy about it! I still got the feeling Claudia had wanted her mum to come home – but you could never really tell where you were with her. Anyway, Bethan and Claudia seemed to be spending more time together, and both seemed very content. Their new friendship reminded me a bit of those parasitic relationships – you know, like tiny fish living on the back of sharks. Bethan could spread Claudia's endless juicy stories about her love life around Year Ten, and in return Claudia would receive a constant stream of attention. Meanwhile, Poppy and I had decided not to have a big fight with Claudia. She would find it most difficult of all if we just left her to it.

Sasha came up to me. 'Chocolate?'

I took a square. Yum. Then she ran off to offer Charlotte some as well. Sasha and I had made up in the end, when she phoned me one night out of the blue. She had been totally traumatised because she'd sent Darren a really juicy text message, but accidentally sent it to the person before Darren in her mobile.

'Who?' I had said.

'My dad,' Sasha had said woefully.

With that, I had laughed and she had laughed. And we had both said sorry.

Poppy came up to me, zigzagging.

'Why are you doing that?' I said. 'It's not raining.'

'I know, but it keeps me warm,' said Poppy. 'Anyway, I've got something to tell you!'

'What?' I said. We both looked around to check Bethan still wasn't within earshot.

Poppy looked thrilled. 'I got together with Jez!'

Oh my God!

'He called me last night! You know, we had got talking at Fireworks Night. And he said he was passing my house so he came over and . . .'

'You kissed?'

She nodded and beamed with suppressed delight. 'Not only that, he took two of the chocolate Christmas decorations from our tree and put them on my ears, like earrings!'

'That's so romantic!'

I guess there had been one good thing to come out of Claudia going on the Big Wheel with Luke: it had left Poppy and Jez to talk. Finally!

'He said he's always liked me, ever since we met!' said Poppy. 'And he's going to show me how to rollerblade, and . . .'

Then she stopped. 'Sorry,' she said. 'I'm a bit obsessed at the moment!'

'Is Jez going to come along for Christmas Eve?' I asked.

Poppy and I had agreed to meet up and exchange Christmas presents on Christmas Eve. After all, you had to spend Christmas Day with your family, but Christmas Eve was a bit different. I had finally figured out that it was OK that there were no pheromones for friends. You were free to choose your friends. And the fact that you had friends through choice, not biology, seemed to indicate they were just as special. If not more so.

'No,' said Poppy. 'Maybe Jez can do something with Luke!'

'Where is Mrs Mastiff?' I said. After all, it may have been sunny, but it was freezing cold.

'Susanna Forbes went to the staffroom to find out,' said Poppy.

Typical.

That was when Susanna appeared from the school building. She called out something indistinct.

'What did she say?' I asked.

'Something about it being cold,' said Bethan.

Poppy peered at Susanna and said slowly, 'No, Mrs Mastiff has got a cold.'

A cold!

When Susanna got closer we made her repeat it and it was true. Mrs Mastiff had got a cold after our last netball lesson, and Mrs Craignish had told Susanna we could have free time!

A few people stayed outside in their PE kit. Poppy and I zigzagged together back to the locker rooms, which for some reason gave us both a really bad fit of the giggles.

'Where are you going once you've got changed?' said Poppy, once we'd recovered. 'Can I come?'

'Of course,' I said, still aching from the laughter. All that laughing had given me a stitch. I was going to the library to do my Extra English, and maybe pick out a new DVD for Poppy and me to watch on Christmas Eve. Something with a happy ending.

THE END

Find out how it all started!

In the back of my rough book I wrote a list of hurdles I needed to overcome in order to meet Luke and some of his friends in town for an almost-date type situation.

1. *Get Poppy to invite Jez.*
2. *Phone Luke (ignoring obvious further hurdle of family listening in while I talk on landline).*
3. *Possibly clarify to Luke who I am.*
4. *Present compelling reasons as to why Luke would want to agree to the above, along with his friends, whom I've never met.*

Meet Holly Stockwell, fourteen. She hates all forms of exercise, gets tongue-tied around boys, and her best friend, Poppy, seems to be developing a *new* best friend – the rich and gorgeous Claudia! Can she overcome these traumas without life getting any worse?

ISBN: 978 1 85340 851 9

. . . and then what happened!

'Listen – Luke just kissed me!'
'Oh my God!' Poppy shrieked. She repeated, incredulously,
'Luke?' 'Yes, Luke. You know? Your brother? Picture in the
dictionary under "gorgeous"? Just imagine telling everyone at
school.' Maybe that was the wrong thing to be considering,
but it had never happened to me before – you know, that
thing where you run into school with show-stopping,
jaw-dropping news and everyone crowds round you
and gets all distracted in assembly.

Finally Luke seems to have noticed that Holly is not just his
sister's best friend! But, before anything else can happen, Holly
and Poppy go off to Cornwall for a group camping holiday.

Will Luke be waiting for Holly when she gets back? And, when
having the right image seems so important, will Holly be brave
enough to drop the camouflage and be herself?

ISBN: 978 1 85340 913 4

www.piccadillypress.co.uk

☆ The latest news on forthcoming books

☆ Chapter previews

☆ Author biographies

☆ Fun quizzes

☆ Reader reviews

☆ Competitions and fab prizes

☆ Book features and cool downloads

☆ And much, much more . . .

Log on and check it out!

Piccadilly Press